The Further Adventures Of Daisy Miller

A NOVELLA

Lawrence Kessenich

Daisy Miller Lives! One of the most alluring and enigmatic of Henry James's Americans Abroad, Daisy survives the "Roman fever" in Lawrence Kessenich's playful and insightful sequel to the famous James novella, and – finally! – gets a chance to explain herself.

Daisy, eventually meeting up with her loyal if long-suffering admirer Frederick Winterbourne, has fled the viperous tongues of Roman society and landed in the Paris of the Exposition Universelle, of John Singer Sargent and of romantic, post-Montgolfier ballooning rides.

I know you'll enjoy this sly, literate and insightful postlude to one of the greatest unfinished love stories of modern fiction.

Alex Beam

Boston Globe columnist, author of
The Americans Are Coming! and ***Fellow Travelers***

At last Daisy Miller gets the life she deserves--not dead of Roman fever, but fully alive: immersing herself in the pleasures of late nineteenth-century Paris, charming everyone she meets with her vivacity, and ultimately devoting herself to the cause of women's liberation. This sequel to Henry James's 1878 novella is as appealing as its heroine—full of lively conversation and period detail.

Ruth Hoberman

Professor emerita, English, Eastern Illinois University
Author of ***Museum Trouble: Edwardian Fiction***
And The Emergence Of Modernism.

Good news: reports of Daisy Miller's death, it turns out, were greatly exaggerated. In resurrecting Henry James' fetching ingenue, Lawrence Kessenich has done the literary world a favor, supplying Daisy this time out not only with a pen to correct Mr. James' misapprehensions, but with a derringer pistol for the wrong sort of fellow, those "unwilling to be discouraged." Enjoyable, witty, well-written—and ultimately quite serious—this feminist Daisy has her heart and values in the right place, and so does this novel.

David Payne
Author of ***Confessions Of A Taoist On Wall Street*** and ***Barefoot To Avalon***

First Edition, April 2025
Library of Congress Control Number: *pending*
ISBN 978-1-965784-14-3 Hardback
ISBN 978-1-965784-15-0 Paperback

Cover Design by Kurt Lovelace
Cover Artwork by Pierian Springs Press
Cover type *Bauhaus Dessau* Alfarn by Céline Hurka,
Elia Preuss, Flavia Zimbardi,
Hidetaka Yamasaki, and Luca Pellegrini.
Body & Chapter Titles set in **No 9T**
Headers in **Jenson** by Robert Slimbach
Flourishes set in Emigre Foundry **Dalliance**,
by Frank Heine & Emigre Foundry **ZeitGuys**,
by Bob Aufuldish, Eric Donelan.
Typefaces licensed Adobe, Linotype, Emigre, & URW GmbH.

PSPress.Pub
Pierian Springs Press, Inc
30 N Gould St, Ste 25398
Sheridan, Wyoming 82801-6317

"I have never allowed a gentleman to dictate to me, or to interfere with anything I do."

HENRY JAMES
Daisy Miller

The Further Adventures Of Daisy Miller

1

DAISY

Mr. James was wrong. I did not die of the Roman fever, although I was indeed deathly ill for some time. He must have left Rome assuming I was on my way out of this world, but I was far from done with my adventures. I faced down the fever just as I'd faced down Mrs. Walker, after she snubbed me at her party, not long before I got ill. It did wound me in the moment, I will admit, but I ain't one to dwell on small slights. Heaven knows it would have been like the Chinese death by a thousand cuts if I had dwelt on the way my fellow Americans treated me in Rome.

I am proud to be an American from Schenectady, New York, but sometimes I find my countrymen Puritanical to a disturbing degree. What is to be gained from suppressing every natural instinct in order to uphold a completely arbitrary set of rules about how to behave? As I see it, God gave us life to live it—not to hedge it about on all sides with unnecessary rules. I enjoy the company of men—many and various men. I enjoy being alone with them, and I believe I ought to be trusted to do that. That said, I am not naïve, though many, including Mr. Winterbourne, think me so. I am well aware of the lustful desires men harbor and always firmly discourage them from acting on those desires. I also carry a derringer pistol, in case I encounter a man unwilling to be discouraged. It has not happened, yet, because I am usually able to read men and so avoid the type, but I am not foolish enough to think it couldn't happen. So, I go about prepared. But I go about as I wish, and will not stop doing so.

When the doctor had done all he could, and I started to recover from the Roman fever, mother nursed me back to health. Unlike me, mother is hopelessly adrift in society, but in our rooms, where she is comfortable, she is capable of great love and care—as is my father back home. (I do miss Papa so.) I believe it is their love and care throughout my childhood that gave me the belief in myself, the confidence, to move about in society on my own terms. And perhaps mother's lack of awareness about how society functions prevented my becoming a victim of its petty proscriptions. Father is also a man of the world, and I believe I imbibed his confidence in that sphere. So, I am comfortable among people—even those who may not be comfortable with me—and as I recovered from the Roman fever I found myself once again wanting to be among new and interesting people.

Another impression given by Mr. James was that I was only interested in spending time with men. I will admit that I have the usual desire of a young woman my age to be admired and entertained by men—perhaps even an unusual degree of that desire—but I also value female companionship. Mr. James didn't bother to chronicle my outings with female friends, perhaps because it didn't serve the purpose of showing a woman disobedient to the rules of male-female companionship getting her just deserts. But I had at the time, and continue to have, many female friends. After all, what is the good of spending time with men, if you can't discuss them with your female friends afterward? Not that—by any means—men are all we talk about, as much as men might wish they were our sole concern. Life is too rich a feast to focus on one dish.

2

WINTERBOURNE

Mr. James got it wrong—or otherwise altered the facts to suit his story. When I left Rome, Daisy Miller was still alive, although she was reportedly so ill that it was assumed she would pass on shortly. I traveled to Paris to distract myself from her impending death with opera and theatre and music, because what I thought was her parting message about not being engaged had made me realize that I was in love with her—despite her mad disregard for social norms, deeply in love with her. She had a freshness, an uncompromising belief in her own instincts, that I found fascinating, that made me question whether or not I was truly self-confident and sincere in my own dealings with others. But I was enough of a creature of Boston society, and of the Swiss society in which I had spent a good portion of my life, to realize that there could be no future with a woman who lived so far outside the norms of that society. I was a man of my place and time and was not mentally equipped to challenge those norms as she did.

Still, when I learned that Daisy Miller was still alive my heart leapt. My aunt, Mrs. Costello, sent a letter full of outrage that God had let such a creature endure on the earth—by which she meant her particular corner of the earth—when much more civilized women died daily. It had almost shaken her faith in the Almighty. But I must admit that it *strengthened* my faith. Perhaps God appreciated such creatures more than we did. The thought that Miss Miller still walked the earth thrilled me more than I wanted to admit. I only wished that I could have achieved a God-like tolerance for her behavior. If I had, I would have hurried back to her in Rome immediately. As it was, I consoled myself with the thought that God had removed me from a place of temptation, where I might have involved myself too deeply with an ungovernable creature, one sure to bring discord into my life.

3

DAISY

Nothing changed after my recovery. I foolishly hoped that my near death would soften the attitudes of my fellow Americans in Rome, but it seemed, instead, that they were disappointed I had survived—especially when I returned to my old ways. Mr. Giovanelli hadn't dared to approach my mother about being allowed to see me while I was ill, thinking that she, like Mr. Winterbourne, would blame him for my escapade in the Colosseum. But he appeared at our doorstep the moment word got out that I was healthy again. I was touched by the great joy he expressed at my recovery, and moved, on our very first outing—to my favorite Pincio garden, with its grand view of the city—by his offer to marry me. He asked about it in a way that indicated he expected to be refused, and I did not disappoint him. Much as I loved his company, I was not *in love* with him, and I planned to settle for no less when—if—I finally decided to marry. He was sad for a few hours afterward, but, like a true Italian, he soon refocused on the joy of the moment, on our being together again, for however long it would last. If only Mr. Winterbourne had imbibed that attitude toward me—and life—as a result of spending time in Rome, we might have made jolly companions.

The American community in Rome being what it was, I decided it was time to move on to another city, and Paris, which I had never visited, came immediately to mind. Surely, I thought, Americans in that great bastion of free thought would be less constrained—and constraining—than those in Rome. I convinced mother and Randolph that we should go there by emphasizing that the Exposition Universelle was opening on May 1st. In addition to the attractiveness of the exposition, we had often been told that no city compares to Paris in the springtime, so this seemed like the ideal time to go. It was decided (mother would say that I decided) that we would leave Rome in mid-April. I could hardly wait!

4

WINTERBOURNE

In the event, I was unable to escape Daisy Miller. Perhaps this was the Devil's revenge on God for moving me away from such a temptation. It was as if he were taunting God—and me—saying, "Ach, it is easy enough to resist temptation that is nearly a thousand miles away, but much more difficult when it is close at hand." I was at a performance of La Traviata at the new Paris Opera House, sitting in a balcony seat beside the stage, which afforded an excellent view of the audience, when my eyes lighted upon Miss Miller, sitting with her mother a few rows back from the front. At first, I was convinced that my eyes deceived me, that she couldn't possibly be alive and in Paris, but then I realized that if anyone had the pluck to survive the Roman fever, it was Daisy Miller. And there was no reason they would not have traveled from Rome to one of the other great cities of Europe.

It took only a moment of observing that uniquely pretty and lively face to realize that it could be no one else. I was both thrilled and horrified. That face moved me like no other, but the mobile, free, and easy quality of her expressions brought back her utter disregard for the way things are normally done in society. In fact, I observed the gentleman and lady in front of her frequently turning their heads to see what kind of creature had chosen to sit behind them, and their countenances conveyed the surprise and disapproval that so often greeted Miss Miller's public behavior.

I should have left it alone. I had not been planning to stay in Paris much longer, and I should have left. But I did not. I simply could not. Whatever problems might arise from reassociating myself with Daisy Miller, I had to be in her magnetic presence again, had to ascertain how she was getting on after her illness and in a new city.

I could not resist even for the entirety of the opera, but sought her out during the intermission. She stood with her mother, sipping champagne, her ever-curious eyes dancing over the fashionable crowd parading before her. She looked entirely happy. And I do not think I flatter myself when I say that she looked even happier when her eyes lighted upon me as I approached.

"Why, Mr. Winterbourne," she said before I could speak. "What are the chances that we would renew our acquaintance in The City of Lights? It certainly lights up my evening to lay eyes on you again."

As usual, I was completely nonplussed by the level of familiarity and affection inherent in the way Miss Miller spoke to me. It was as if she were greeting a lifelong friend, someone of great significance to her, not a casual acquaintance of a few months. I felt honored to think that perhaps she matched my level of affection for her.

"Good evening, Miss Miller, Mrs. Miller. It does my heart good to see you not only alive, Miss Miller, but apparently healthy and strong."

"I am indeed healthy and strong, Mr. Winterbourne. I've even regained the scandalous amount of weight I lost while suffering from the Roman fever. It was a great trial, but mother nursed me back to health, and here I am before you."

Mrs. Miller mumbled protestations about having nothing to do with her daughters recovery, without meeting Winterbourne's gaze.

"What brings you to Paris?" I inquired.

"I might ask the same of you, sir. You deserted me on my sickbed, and I was sure you'd gone back to your lady friend in Geneva. But here you are in Paris—on your own, I take it, since no lady accompanies you."

I had forgotten Miss Miller's talent for putting me off balance with her bold statements. I was speechless for a moment.

"Come, now, Mr. Winterbourne. Surely you can entertain a young lady recently arisen from her deathbed with news of your social activities. I've been starved for stories about people out and about in the world."

"If you must know, my Geneva friend and I have parted ways. I came to Paris to distract myself from that and, I will be honest with you, mourn your passing from this world, which appeared imminent when I left Rome."

"And yet, here I am, back to taunt you. You must enjoy the taunting if you went to the trouble of seeking me out during the intermission."

How did she know that I'd come looking for her and hadn't just happened upon her? As usual, Miss Miller mysteriously deduced things about my behavior that I hadn't intended to reveal. She really was an extraordinary young woman. And, although it seemed she was no less lively, playful, and bold than she had been before her illness, I sensed a new gravity, a solidity about her that had not been there before. Previously, it had seemed as if she were as light as a bird in flight, flitting from place to place, person to person, topic to topic—so light that she could be blown about haphazardly by the wind. Now, she seemed more like a beautiful bird resting on a branch, gripping it firmly, enjoying the view, and singing merrily.

To divert the conversation away from Miss Miller's statement about my enjoying being taunted, I asked Mrs. Miller what had brought *her* to Paris. She turned her head nervously to me for a moment, but looked away as she answered.

"I'm sure I don't know. It's all Daisy's doing. Some exposition or other and something about spring."

"The spring is lovely here," I said. "And I am looking forward to the exposition, myself—as is all of Paris."

"You must take us, then!" exclaimed Miss Miller. "Presumably you know your way around Paris—and Parisians—much better than we do. Oh, that would be so thoughtful of you!"

How could I refuse that lovely young woman anything?

"If I am still in Paris when you want to go, I would be delighted to escort you."

"If you're still in Paris? Well, you certainly can't leave, now that your dear friend has risen from the grave and come to visit you."

The way she said this, I almost believed that she had come to Paris for my sake, despite the fact that she'd had no idea I would be there. Such are the bewitching powers of Miss Daisy Miller.

"I charge you to procure tickets for me, mother, Randolph, and yourself, Mr. Winterbourne. It's the least you can do to celebrate my miraculous resurrection."

"It will be my pleasure."

5

DAISY

I had an inkling that Mr. Winterbourne was suffering more from the end of his relationship with the Geneva woman than he let on—perhaps even to himself. I have perceived from the first that he has but a nodding acquaintance with his feelings. He seems more English than American in this way—the stiff upper lip and all that. Not that American men are free with their emotions, but perhaps a bit freer than the English, who, after all, have a grand empire to maintain, which must demand a great deal of self-control. But I would get the truth about things with the Geneva woman out of Mr. Winterbourne. Most men yield to my curiosity eventually.

Good as his word, Mr. Winterbourne bought us all tickets for the marvelous Exposition Universelle, refusing to let us pay for our own, and we set out in an open carriage early on a lovely Wednesday morning, a day chosen to avoid the larger crowds on the weekend. Randolph could hardly sit still, he was so excited to see everything: the animal statues, the hot air balloons, the hall of machines, the underground aquarium. I looked forward to all of those, myself, as well as the art work and home furnishings, the international pavilions, and the exotic foods. Even mother, who was not an enthusiastic walker, was excited enough about the exposition to take on the strenuous day—in fact, shedding her reticence, she seemed nearly as excited as Randolph. Mr. Winterbourne was his usual phlegmatic self, not revealing what he felt about the excursion. Being with me seemed to be his primary interest, and I could hardly blame him for that. I hoped that my enthusiasm about the exposition would eventually ignite his own.

The carriage let us off before the imposing columns of the Trocadero Palace, which invoked the Colosseum in Rome. But jutting up high above them were Moorish towers that were, I'd read in the newspaper, forty-five feet taller than the towers of Notre Dame! A columned arcade swept out in a grand curve from each side of the main structure. Architects had criticized the building's pastiche of styles, but for me it all worked together to seem both imposing and inviting.

Before we entered the building, Randolph was released to explore the many bronze animal sculptures in front of it. As is her habit, mother let him roam at will, and it wasn't until he called to us from the back of a giant bull on a tall pedestal that she realized a little more supervision might be in order in this setting. Wanting to see the exposition grounds before exploring any particular buildings, we passed through the Trocadero and out into the beautiful gardens that were embraced by the two arcades. Trees and plants grew in profusion beside the circuitous walkways and immense columns of water spouted from great pools of water. At the opposite end of the gardens, a metal bridge crossed the Seine, leading to the main grounds of the exposition. I noticed that the entrance to the underground aquarium was nearby and was about to tell Randolph, but when I looked up he was already half way to the bridge, running as fast as he could. Mother was hurrying after him, ordering him to stop and wait for us at the bridge. So, the aquarium would have to wait.

This left Mr. Winterbourne and I alone together. I took his arm and we strolled toward the bridge.

"It's very good of you to bring us all here," I said.

"It is my distinct pleasure," he replied.

"Were you *very* surprised to see me at the opera?"

"It was as if you had risen from the dead, as if I were witnessing a miracle. I was so shocked that I lost my breath for a moment."

"But you recovered quickly and came to find me."

"I did indeed."

"Were you *very* happy that I was still alive?"

"I don't believe I've ever been happier."

"I enjoy it when you say things like that."

"Then I will say more of them."

"Do you miss your Geneva lady?"

Mr. Winterbourne blushed to roots of his hair.

"Your questions are very bold, Miss Miller."

"You have known that about me since you first met me, Mr. Winterbourne. Surely you didn't expect even a near-death experience to alter that aspect of my behavior."

Now, he smiled.

"I have become unused to your ways in the interim since our time together in Rome."

"Are you *very* sorry for the way you treated me there?"

"The way *I* treated you? I was one of your few defenders."

"Until you found me in the Colosseum at midnight with Mr. Giovanelli."

Again he blushed, but less this time.

"You seem to enjoy testing the boundaries of propriety, Miss Miller. I am not accustomed to women who do that."

"Did your Geneva lady adhere more strictly to the social code?"

"If you must know, yes. She was comfortably conventional."

"And yet she was seeing you, a much younger man."

"How did you know... I cannot fathom you, Miss Miller. It seems you know all of my secrets. There is nothing wrong with a young man courting an older woman."

"But it's hardly conventional."

For a moment, Mr. Winterbourne stared off at the playing fountain we were passing. Then he looked back at me.

"No, perhaps not conventional—but certainly not improper."

I laughed.

"It is that kind of hairsplitting that makes the rules of society ridiculous to me. Who is to say that this behavior is right and that behavior is wrong? It seems to me that if people followed their true instincts and conscience they would know what is naturally proper and improper."

"You trust individuals too much, my dear."

"I would rather trust them too much than too little."

By this time we had reached the bridge and found mother holding onto my little brother for dear life.

"They're here, now, mother," said Randolph. "Let me go!"

"Only if you promise to walk, not run, and to stay in our sight."

"I promise, I promise—now let me go!"

Mother released her grip and, good boy that he basically is, Randolph began walking ahead—quickly, but not running—toward the Palais du Champ-de-Mars' Gallerie du machines, with its promise of great mechanical wonders. We increased our speed to keep up with him.

The gallery was built of arched glass supported by metal beams and was nearly as tall as a cathedral, symbolizing, it seemed to me, industry as the new religion of the Western world. Below this vast expanse of glass were machines of all shapes and sizes, some small and compact, others incorporating metal wheels the size of elephants. Some of them were in motion, creating fearful sounds that bounced off the surrounding glass. It was a bit much for me, but Randolph was in his glory.

6

WINTERBOURNE

I had, of course, always enjoyed the company of Daisy Miller, but I'd had little interaction with her brother, Randolph. At the Gallerie du machines, however, we shared a fascination with the products of Western industry. He stared at the mechanical beasts as if they were the wonders of the world, which, in a way, I suppose they are. I had never seen him stand still for so long. He begged me, because I had better French than his mother or sister, to translate the descriptions of what each machine was and how it worked. The hall contained everything from a small "typewriter," a machine that allowed the user to impress words on paper, letter by letter, to an immense steam locomotive, suspended from underneath so that it's great wheels could be set in motion.

Spending time with Randolph stole time I would have spent alongside Miss Miller, but, truth be told, I was content to have some relief from her inquiries about my friend in Geneva. She had no tact whatsoever when it came to asking personal questions, and it made me uncomfortable. It seemed that whenever I was with that young woman, I alternated between being utterly fascinated by her and utterly appalled by things she said and did.

The most exciting objects in the hall, I am proud to say, were the inventions of our own Mr. Edison. I had already witnessed his astounding electric lighting at a demonstration in the city. His lights had been installed all along the Avenue de l'Opera and the Place de l'Opera, and when a switch was thrown on a dark, moonless night, it lit those streets with a brilliance that made gaslight look pale, virtually banishing the night! Here at the exposition, his megaphone for the hard-of-hearing astonished us, amplifying sound significantly—fifty times, the exhibitors claimed. But the *pièce de resistance* was his phonograph, a simple mechanical device that used a mouthpiece for activating a notched disk, which in turn made indentations on tinfoil wrapped around a brass cylinder as the user spoke. Once a voice was recorded, it could, to our astonishment, be played back, repeating what the user had said. It was utterly magical, and all of us were as giddy as children witnessing the magic.

Miss Miller was particularly demonstrative in her reaction to this device, and in that reaction I saw the charming, highly curious little girl she must have been, taking delight in every new experience life put before her. I suppose it was natural for such a soul to carry this attitude into relations with men, but it seemed to me a very dangerous transfer of something childlike to an adult setting. I felt most protective of her in that moment, although I knew she was convinced that she had no need of my protection. I resolved to convince her that this was not true.

We spent so long in the Gallerie du machines that, when we finally completed our tour, it was time for lunch. We chose a grand buffet that allowed Randolph, a notoriously fussy eater, to choose only the foods that appealed to him. We sat on a shaded terrace to eat, grateful to be off our feet for a time. From there, we could see the brightly colored hot air balloons in the distance, which excited Randolph so much that he could barely be convinced to eat his lunch. When we were done, we went immediately to the balloons and joined the long line waiting to ascend in them. Fortunately, the balloon baskets were quite large and held many people, so the line progressed quickly. Also, there were several balloons, and all they did was rise on a tether—although to a point higher than the Moorish towers on the Trocadero, it must be said—so the "ride" did not take too long.

Once we were entered the basket—Randolph hurrying ahead to secure us a position at the edge—and it was filled with people, the captain of the vessel ordered the tethers loosed and the hot air made the balloon rise. It is the closest thing to flight that human beings are capable of experiencing, thrilling all of us. Until we reached the end of our tether, at which point Miss Miller expressed her disappointment.

"It's unfortunate that they've constrained us so. I would dearly love to fly out across the city, high above the Seine and the Tuileries and the towers of Notre Dame. It would be magnificent!"

"Such flights are available for a price," I said. "Perhaps I will take you one day."

"Would you, really? I would be most indebted to you for such an adventure. So much more exciting than our tour of Chateau de Chillon in Switzerland!"

"My goodness," said Mrs. Miller. "You would never convince *me* to fly unfettered below an immense balloon over Paris. I would be terrified!"

Fortunately, young Randolph was so preoccupied with looking down on the exposition grounds and city that he didn't hear my offer, for I knew he would have no qualms about such a flight either, and, selfishly, it was an adventure I very much wanted to share alone with Miss Miller.

After the balloon ascension, we went the other direction, downward into the underground aquarium. Arched corridors with rough plaster walls and stalagmites led to lit glass tanks imbedded into the rough plaster, looking as if someone had dug through the earth and found themselves deep below the surface of a sea or lake. Multicolored fish and other water creatures moved about languidly in the water and sometimes approached the glass to stare back at us.

"I wonder who is observing whom," said Miss Miller, and laughed heartily.

The dark underground chambers and the languid fish had a calming effect on Randolph, who simply stared at the creatures and occasionally asked me what one of them was called. And Mrs. Miller was even quieter than she had been, if that is possible. I thought she was probably getting tired of walking—which she confirmed as we took the water pressure powered elevator from the aquarium to the surface.

"Randolph, my son," she said, "it is time for you to take your mother home."

Surprisingly, he acquiesced, apparently tired himself.

"All right, mother," he said. "But I must come back someday. There is ever so much to see."

I assured him that I would bring him back, and then Miss Miller and I saw them off in the carriage. I instructed my driver to return to the Trocadero in a few hours and wait for us.

It was delicious to have Miss Miller to myself—although I must confess that she took so much interest in everything and everyone she encountered that it was sometimes hard to credit that she felt the same way about being with me. As we wandered the grounds, she would strike up an animated conversation with virtually anyone—a street musician, a storekeeper, a policemen, someone running one of the food carts that lined certain walkways—and, even with her rudimentary French, seemed to make each of them feel as special as she made me feel. I found it difficult not to be jealous.

We viewed the art and home furnishings displays and many of the exotic pavilions from countries around the world. Miss Miller took a vivid interest in everything we encountered—for instance, furnishing virtually the entire house she imagined in her future with paintings, statuary, and fine furniture, and even choosing wallpaper designs that pleased her. She also enjoyed being surprised by the way people in other cultures lived, as evidenced by the displays in their pavilions.

"I will travel widely, one day, Mr. Winterbourne—you mark my words. Europe is fine, but I want China and India and Africa, places where the way of life is so very different from our own. Would you accompany me on my exotic journeys, or are Switzerland and Italy and France enough for you?"

Again, Miss Miller had intuited something about me that I would rather not reveal, which was that I did not have much taste for the exotic and was somewhat fearful of exotic travel. But I could hardly unman myself in front of her by admitting such a thing.

"I believe I would follow you to the ends of the earth, Miss Miller."

"Excellent answer, Mr. Winterbourne. However, it reveals more about what you feel for *me* than for exotic travel. But it is so complimentary that I will let you escape this time."

And I realized in that moment that I *would* follow this young woman anywhere, even to places where I might feel uncomfortable.

"Speaking of exotic experiences, sir, did you mean it when you offered to take me on a balloon ride far above the city?"

"Of course."

"Then I propose that we dedicate this very afternoon to that adventure. Are you with me, Mr. Winterbourne?"

"Your wish is my command."

"Then I command you to take me flying!"

7

DAISY

It was most generous of Mr. Winterbourne to indulge me with a balloon ride. I will admit to having felt a twinge of anxiety at the thought of flying unfettered across the Parisian sky, but I have found that the most rewarding experiences are those that both attract me strongly and frighten me a bit. So, engage a balloon we did. In the same area where the balloons with large baskets took many people up and down, there were also several for hire with much smaller baskets. The price included a carriage ride back to the exposition at the end of the flight, of course, because the balloons were propelled only by the wind, in whatever direction it was blowing, so we could not have flown back to the exposition without circling the earth—as in Mr. Verne's *Around the World in Eighty Days*. Now, that was an adventure I envied!

Our balloon was a bright red—my favorite color—and the basket had room for just me, Mr. Winterbourne, and our captain, the handsome Ms. Petit. Naturally, I flirted with him, and naturally Mr. Winterbourne was peevish because of this. But I dedicated much more of my attention to him than to the captain, so I don't see why he was jealous. Men—including Mr. Winterbourne—have no compunction about eyeing every pretty woman they pass on the street, so I see no reason why women should be denied such an innocent pleasure. Humans are animals, after all, and males and females can't help sniffing around each other.

Other than Mr. Winterbourne's mild pique—which, to his credit, he mastered in relatively short order—the ride was magnificent. I had, of course, stood on mountains and looked down on people and objects that looked like toys, but there is something about seeing such things from a vehicle suspended in the sky and moving through the air that makes it that much more exciting. It was as if we were royalty, borne aloft by the gods to survey our realm and our subjects, most of whom paused their activity and waved to us. My arm was sore from waving back by the time the journey ended.

In the narrow space of the basket, Mr. Winterbourne took the opportunity to stand very close to me, which provided an excitement of its own. I can't quite pin down what it was about a man who could be so deucedly conservative that attracted me. He did listen to me in a way that few men ever have—save dear Mr. Giovanelli in Rome, although part of Mr. G's rapt attention may be assigned to his striving to understand my English and pitiful Italian—and there is nothing a woman, or for that matter a man, enjoys more than truly being listened to. I also saw Mr. Winterbourne struggling to understand, and therefore not condemn, my unusual social behavior, as he has from the day he met me. And I give credit to any man for trying, when so many men dismiss women as the weaker and stupider sex. And, patronizing though it could be, at times, his desire to protect me was endearing.

The balloon ride, which ended all too quickly, brought us to the outskirts of Paris, where we landed nearly *in* the carriage awaiting to return us to the exposition. I complimented Ms. Petit on his skill with the balloon, and Mr. Winterbourne grudgingly seconded my compliment. Then we were in the carriage on our way back into the city. When we arrived at the exposition, it was time for supper, and Mr. Winterbourne told me to choose where we would eat. Of course, I chose the exotic, an open air Moorish restaurant with waiters in fezzes and vests and ballooning red silk pantaloons. We sat on large, firm pillows on the floor and ate with our hands, pinching things between thumb and forefinger in the Moroccan style shown us by the waiter. At first, Mr. Winterbourne was nonplussed by this unfamiliar posture and way of eating, but he warmed to it as we drank wine to accompany the food—French wine, the Moroccans being Mohammedans and therefore abstaining from the production of alcohol. We shared a variety of small dishes—couscous, lamb, chicken with vegetables, boiled eggs—and ended with sweet plums and dark coffee. In the end, we were both very happy, with our food and with each other, so our day ended on a positive note.

8

WINTERBOURNE

An afternoon alone with Miss Miller is both wonderful and agonizing. I often fear that she is playing with my affections, but I always come to the conclusion that she is simply following her unbridled nature, which causes her to say and do things I am wholly unused to. I was not wrong when I surmised early on that she resembled a "typical" American flirt in her actions, but that behavior is not an affectation with her. It is simply an expression of her appreciation for the richness of life. The fact that that richness includes handsome men other than myself pains me at times, but ultimately it becomes clear that she is not trying to *make* me jealous; she is just enjoying life. Her way of being seems to be more acceptable to the French, but as we have thus far spent little time within the American community in Paris, I don't not know how she will be viewed there.

But I digress. It was a perfect afternoon, sunny and breezy and dry, and Miss Miller was the perfect companion with whom to enjoy new adventures. She relishes life in a way that makes me feel stodgy, so I do my best to cooperate with her exciting whims, such as the balloon journey and the exotic supper, and let myself go a little. The idea that the life of this exquisite creature could have ended in the bloom of youth in Rome made cooperating with whatever she desired all the easier. She was not a woman to take life in half measures, but rather, as the Bible puts it, "in good measure, pressed down, and shaken together, and running over."

We were so happy and comfortable together after the Moroccan dinner and a bottle of wine that, as we strolled away from the restaurant, arm in arm, I chanced a question I thought might make *her* uncomfortable, for a change. After all, why should *she* be the only one free to do that?

"Miss Miller, there is something I've been meaning to ask you ever since I had the pleasure of discovering you were alive."

"Oh, my. That sounds important. Is it a question I will like?"

"That is for you to say."

"Then fire away."

"I received a message from you via your mother, as you lay on what everyone assumed was your deathbed, saying that you wanted me to know that you were not, in fact, engaged to Mr. Giovanelli."

Here Miss Miller withdrew her arm from mine and blushed significantly—something I had not seen before—but I continued.

"Why was it so important to you that I know that?"

"Mr. Winterbourne, are you fishing for a compliment? I would think it obvious why a young woman would want a young man to know she was not otherwise engaged."

"It was my fond hope that you were communicating some level of affection for me, because I feel a great deal of affection for you."

We continued on toward the Trocadero Palais and the waiting carriage in silence for a few moments. My heart was pounding and my head spinning—and not only because of the wine. Finally, Miss Miller spoke.

"I do indeed have a degree of affection for you, Mr. Winterbourne, and appreciate that you have the same for me. As to whether or not we are temperamentally suited for one other, I am not entirely sure, and I sense that you aren't either."

"As always, you speak the truth," I replied. "But I hope we will continue to spend time together, so that we may ascertain if we are suited to each other or not. I will admit to some hesitation about your way of being in society, but I care for you enough to test my ability to go along with you on your unorthodox path—or your ability to adjust to my more orthodox path. I hope that we may spend time together regularly here in Paris, so that we may, as the saying goes, test our affections."

Without saying more, Miss Miller took my arm back —which I saw as agreement with my proposal—and we proceeded to the carriage.

9
DAISY

I do care for Mr. Winterbourne. What level of caring I might reach is an open question. We are in some ways so unsuited, though of late we seemed to be growing more in each other's direction. He is showing himself more keen to follow me on little adventures and I am trying to be more open to his need for a certain level of propriety.

But then Mrs. Claiborne, the acknowledged "queen" of the American contingent in Paris, held a party, to which he and I were both invited, individually. As was often her wont with parties, mother decided at the last minute that she had a headache and wouldn't go. So, I went on my own. The first moment of discomfort between Mr. Winterbourne and myself occurred when I entered the party alone. This is the sort of thing—an unmarried woman arriving unescorted to a party—that is "not done" in "good" society, but I wasn't going to miss a fine party just because mother had a headache. Mr. Winterbourne happened to be near the door when I entered, and he looked pained to see me appear alone and embarrassed by the reactions of everyone around him, all of whom looked at me with disdain. Gentleman that he is, he came to my rescue immediately, offering me his arm and escorting me toward the table laden with food and drink. This seemed to relieve some of the tension in the room, but a residue remained, and I caught various people glancing at me with censorious looks.

"Why did you not tell me you required an escort tonight, Miss Miller," said Winterbourne, trying—but not succeeding—to the keep the censure out of his voice.

"Oh, well," I said, "mother decided at the very last minute that she was not up to coming, so I had no choice but to come alone."

"You could have chosen to stay home."

I look at him incredulously.

"Stay home? Is that what you wish I'd done, Mr. Winterbourne? Hardly the warmest welcome."

"I'm not speaking about what *I* want, but what good society dictates."

"Were you allowed to come on your own, Mr. Winterbourne?"

"Of course."

"Then why can't I?

"Because women need protection."

"I would like to know who will protect me from the

slings and arrows of my fellow Americans right here!"

"I think it's all right, now. Since I met you at the door, I'm sure people think you were delayed for some reason and that I am your escort for the evening. I will most certainly see you home."

"I believe you mean to say, 'I'd be delighted to escort you home, should you wish it, Miss Miller.'"

I could see in Mr. Winterbourne's eyes a desire to take me in hand and demand that he see me home. But then his look softened a bit, and he replied in a conciliatory tone.

"I am only concerned for your safety and your reputation, Miss Miller, but naturally you may choose to accept my offer or not."

He was learning. But, of course, I was not testing him—not intentionally; I am not that sort of woman—but simply being my gay self. I met a number of men and women I wanted to converse with alone that evening, and I didn't hesitate to excuse myself to do so. Mr. Winterbourne could hardly constrain me, much as he might have wished to, and I did always circle back to him. But whenever I was away from him, I would catch him glancing at me—frequently if I was with a man—with disapproval in his eyes. The champagne flowed freely at the party, and I enjoyed it, although I am wise enough to keep my head about me. It was good that I had trained myself on Italian wine in Rome, because I had become better at keeping my head, as a result. I knew how to drink at a rate that promoted gaiety without crossing over into foolish or dangerous behavior.

Mrs. Claiborne, the hostess, would have nothing to do with me. Whenever I approached her to say thank you for her lavish party, she suddenly found it necessary to begin conversing with someone else. People such as her and Mrs. Walker in Rome hold themselves up as models of adult behavior, and, yet, both of them behave with the petty peevishness of schoolgirls. Rather than feeling remorse for my own behavior, I was embarrassed for them. I would rather be written out of "good society" than learn to behave in such a childish manner.

10

WINTERBOURNE

Once again, Miss Miller has set herself apart from the American community of which I am a part and with whose members I try to maintain cordial relations. After all, we must band together to present ourselves in the best possible light to foreigners and thereby uphold our national honor. Miss Miller does not seem to grasp this responsibility. Not only did she appear unescorted at Mrs. Claiborne's party, which was attended by a number of Frenchmen, but the very next day she was seen walking the streets unchaperoned with one of the dapper young Frenchman she had met at the party.

Which, of course, wounded my heart. The woman maddens me! One day she expresses affection for me and the next she gambols about with another man. But the fact is, I have no real claim on her and I knew she was bound to do such things in Paris, as she did in Rome. I fantasize about proposing to her, about staking a claim to her affections, but what frightens me is that her behavior might not change as a result of my doing that, which would wound me even more deeply—and our relationship perhaps fatally. Could I really be happy with her, or would I simply be driven mad on a daily basis? This fear holds me back from seriously considering a more formal commitment. I fear I may be like the moth drawn to a bright, hot flame, which will only be immolated it in the end.

But I can't seem to stop seeing her, even if I must get in a queue to do so. As in Rome, Miss Miller is much sought after by young, and older, men of means. She is wined and dined by gentlemen of the best Parisian families, though the word is that none of the families of the younger gentlemen approve of their sons' keeping company with her. And, yet, through all of it, she maintains an air of innocent curiosity and sociability, and when I do see her, she displays not a thread of guilt for enjoying herself as she pleases. Her innocence is real—I will swear to that—which is what keeps me coming back. If I felt she was one of those women who collect men to feed her pride, I would drop her in an instant. But instead of talking of herself, of her conquests, of the flattering things these men say about her, she talks about *them*, their thoughts, their activities, their families. She is clearly not with these men to enhance her vanity, although she enjoys a compliment as much as anyone, but because she is actually *interested* in them as human beings. She speaks of them in the same way she speaks of her female friends—as friends, not as lovers. Which then leads me to fear that she will find one of these men more interesting than I am.

11

DAISY

I have made a new French friend named Alouette, with whom I am able to frankly discuss men. She is as bewildered by them as I am. Like me, she doesn't understand why the sexes are not treated equally, why women are not allowed the same freedom of action and choice that men allow themselves. In fact, Alouette and I met at the International Congress for Women, held in conjunction with the Exposition Universelle. I had never been to anything like it, although I am from upstate New York, the very place where the famous Seneca Falls convention on women's rights was held, several years before I was born. But one has to know people involved in such a movement to learn of it, and neither my mother nor her sisters had any interest in the cause, nor did any of my school friends. I saw a notice about the Congress on a Parisian billboard just as the event was about to end, so I bought a ticket for the final banquet.

It was after the banquet that Alouette and I met, literally bumping into each other as we emerged after Emily Venturi's stirring speech at the end. "Last evening," Venturi had said, "a gentleman who seemed a bit skeptical about the advantages of our Congress asked me, 'Well, Madame, what great truth have you proclaimed to the world?' I replied to him, 'Monsieur, we have proclaimed that woman is a human being.' He laughed. 'But, Madame, that is a platitude.' So it is; but when this platitude, which everyone accepts with a smile when it is merely a question of words, is recognized by human laws, the face of the world will be transformed."

"I wanted to add 'human customs' to 'human laws,' myself," I said to Aloutte, after we struck up a conversation about the speech. "The unspoken customs are as oppressive as the laws."

"Even more so!" said Alouette, "How often does a woman try to divorce or buy a house and run into legal difficulties? But we encounter oppressive customs every day, in every quarter of our life, and they hold us down just as firmly."

I told her the story of Mrs. Claiborne's party and she recognized the situation instantly.

"Men. They so enjoy *their own* social freedom, but somehow become bewildered when *women* want to enjoy the same freedom. Suddenly, it's of no real importance, not something women really need. Ha! It would become important instantly if someone tried to take social freedom away from *them*!"

Alouette and I started meeting once or twice a week for coffee and pastry after that initial encounter, and it was at one of those meetings that I lay before her my dilemma about Mr. Winterbourne.

"What should I do if he ever asks me to become engaged?" I said. "I suspect he both wants to do that and is terrified of doing it."

"Good" said Alouette, "you've frightened him. That's an excellent beginning. He already knows he can't take you for granted, that if he tries to hold onto you too tightly, you will wiggle through his hands and continue to be your own woman, so he's less likely to try. But that only tells you what you might *avoid* with him. What does he offer? We know that men often calculate the value of a match, and we must do the same. What value would there be in it for you?"

A difficult question. As I've said, Mr. Winterbourne does listen to me—really listen, not just nod his head blankly as so many men do when a woman tries to share her thoughts. And, despite his discomfort with the way I socialize with men, he at least seems to realize that I am not a *femme fatale*, but someone who simply enjoys the company of men as much as the company of women. Whether these attitudes would survive his winning my hand is another question. Marriage is hedged on all sides with laws that favor the husband and grant him control over his wife. But I suppose that if I don't get to a place where I trust his good intentions, where I believe he would not be that kind of husband, there would be no point in becoming engaged to him. As Alouette put it, "If the prospect of marrying him makes you fear for your freedom, don't do it! Women have been subject to the whims of men for far too long. Above all, you must be yourself!"

12

WINTERBOURNE

When the magnificent concert hall at the Trocadero Palace was finally completed, months after the rest of the exposition had opened, I escorted Miss Miller to a performance of Strauss waltzes by the Vienna Symphony Orchestra. I would have chosen music with more gravitas—Bach or Beethoven—but she was passionate about waltz music. Apparently, she had first learned ballroom dancing to the music of Strauss, and it brought back all the excitement of those first experiences of an adult activity. In my opinion, it is music that belongs in a ballroom, not a concert hall, but I can see how its beauty and grace reflect Miss Miller's personality, making it meaningful to her no matter where it is performed. Most importantly, it made her happy, and a happy Miss Miller is a pleasure to behold.

Half way through the concert, scarcely able to remain in her seat, she turned to me and whispered in my ear, "Mr. Winterbourne, I believe you should take me out into the aisle and waltz with me."

For a moment, I was horrified, thinking she was serious. But then her eyes twinkled and her smile widened, and she laughed quietly.

"Did I frighten you, Mr. Winterbourne? Even *I* have a better sense of propriety than that. I wouldn't want to induce apoplexy among the more conservative members of the audience."

"Including myself?" I replied.

"You were my first concern. But I must say I find it most difficult to remain seated while these lovely waltz rhythms are played with so much enthusiasm."

"Then you are in luck, Miss Miller. I have been invited to a waltz party at the Sargent's home this very evening, and I am assured it will go late into the night. I refuse to attend without you on my arm."

Her eyes lit up, as I'd hoped they would. It was pure good fortune that this party coincided with the concert, but I will take my luck where I can get it, particularly in connection with anything that pleases Miss Miller. I am not enthusiastic about dancing, myself, but I can hold my own when required, and I would certainly do my best for her.

When the concert ended, Miss Miller seemed to float out of the concert hall, occasionally twirling in a waltz-like manner, and into the waiting carriage. I urged my driver to make haste, and he did as asked, getting us to the Sargent's mansion in less than ten minutes. The home houses the family of John Singer Sargent, a young artist and friend of mine who has just begun painting portraits in Paris. In fact, the ballroom contains portraits of each member of the Sargent family painted by him, and each seems to looked down upon the festivities with restrained gaiety. Mr. Sargent's portraits were not highly emotional, but appreciation for life is reflected in every face.

Miss Miller was given a dance card, and only then did I realize that the ball was attended by a good number of the men who had been seen escorting her around Paris, because as soon as the word was passed that she had arrived, they all competed to get on that card. As I jealously watched her fill it out, I realized that I'd not thought to have her put me on the card. I stood fuming until the gaggle of men attending her had dispersed.

"May I show you my card, Mr. Winterbourne?" she asked, looking as if butter wouldn't melt in her mouth.

"I'm sure I don't need to see an enumeration of how popular you are with men, Miss Miller."

"Oh, I think you do, Mr. Winterbourne. Don't deny me my fun."

Exasperated, I took the card rather roughly from her hand and read it. And there was my name, in the first place on the card, in the middle of the card, and in the last place on the card. She was really quite capable of making a man feel as if he were entirely special to her. I hesitate to admit it, but I nearly teared up. As the next waltz began, she held out her hand to me.

"If you would be kind enough to escort me onto the dance floor, Mr. Winterbourne, I would be most grateful."

She danced with so much grace and enthusiasm, and looked so beautiful in her gown as her skirts rippled and swayed with her movements, that I felt the luckiest man at the ball. I didn't want the dance to end, but of course it did, and then I was forced to step aside while one man after another claimed her to enjoy her grace and beauty on the dance floor. She seemed to bestow on every many who danced with her the same charm and attention she had bestowed on me, which somewhat diminished my sense of being special to her. Trying to hold onto Miss Miller was like trying to pick up mercury. But I resolved to enjoy as much of her attention as she chose to give me, and distracted myself from her exploits by seeking out our host, John Sargent.

"Winterbourne," he said as I approached him, "who is that exquisite creature accompanying you this evening? You have fairly lit up our little gathering by sharing her with us."

"That, John, is Miss Daisy Miller of Schenectady, New York, lately of Vevey, Switzerland and Rome. I had the pleasure of meeting and spending time with her in both of those cities. She is the most extraordinary young woman I have ever met."

"Do I detect a note of passion in the usually dispassionate Frederick Winterbourne?"

"I'm not embarrassed to say that you do."

"Nor should you be. She has *a je ne sais quoi* that is most appealing. I would very much like to paint her. Do you think she would sit for me?"

"Undoubtedly. She is guileless, but she enjoys being admired. The challenge will be getting her to sit still for a portrait."

"Oh, I have ways of relaxing my subjects."

And suddenly I was jealous again. Miss Miller alone with a young, handsome artist who is focusing on her exclusively, who has chosen to fix her beautiful image in oils? I had heard salacious tales about the relationships between artists and their subjects. The situation seemed fraught.

"Well, you may have met your match in Daisy Miller. I'm not sure it would be worth the trouble."

"Pish posh. She will be like putty in my hands."

Which was exactly what I feared.

"You simply *must* introduce me, Winterbourne."

I sighed. Would I ever stop worrying about Miss Miller and other men?

As it turned out, the very next day provided evidence that I would not. Miss Miller had found a new way to scandalize society by strolling casually along the Seine with a married American man, a young industrialist who had moved from Schenectady to Paris for business, bringing his wife and children along. The scandal spread throughout the American community within hours, and the word was that several of our countrymen had immediately uninvited her to various parties and events. Society was swift and vicious in its judgments and actions in response to such transgressions. I felt for Miss Miller—but I also felt exasperated by her. So, I went to her, to both to comfort her and to tell her in no uncertain terms that such behavior must stop, or she would suffer the same fate she had suffered in Rome.

She was, of course, unrepentant.

"A man is a man," she protested, "married or not. A man can have friends. I have known Eddie since we were

young and I am his friend. Anyone who imagines something more in our relationship is making up a fantasy to
indulge their sordid imagination."

"Well, then, most of the American community seems
to be indulging their imagination. I understand that you
are currently welcome nowhere in that community. If
you would only let me guide you in questionable social
circumstance, you could avoid such consequences."

"Are you my father, now? Am I a child to be guided?
In any case, I saw nothing questionable in strolling
about Paris with an old friend—and I still don't. This is
a tempest in a teapot."

"Unfortunately, you live in that teapot, as do I, and I—"

"You feel uncomfortable being associated with a
'scarlet women' who seduces married men. Go on. Be
honest with me."

"This is about you, not me."

"And, yet, here you are, making it your concern."

"My concern is for you, Miss Miller."

"Then you may defend me among your American
friends. Or will that be difficult when you agree with
them?"

"I do not believe that your intentions were bad, but I
do think that meeting him alone showed questionable
judgment."

"And what, pray tell, was questionable? Were our
intentions bad, would we have met in full view of the
public? Meeting privately, secretly, would have indeed
been questionable, but there was nothing questionable
about what we did. When being open and honest is
considered questionable, I doubt the veracity of the
questioner."

The insufferable woman made sense, in her naïve way. But society was not naïve, it was watchful, on guard against inappropriate behavior. It was the bulwark of civilization. It was deuced frustrating to have an inexperienced young woman calling into question the mores of an entire society.

"Sometimes, Miss Miller, in order to get along with our fellow human beings, we need to make concessions, to do things that may not make sense to us as individuals, but which have been adopted by the society in which we live. In order to live there comfortably, we need to conform."

"Then ship me to a desert island, for I have no intention of misshaping myself to fit into a society whose customs I disrespect, whose people seem dedicated to snuffing out every innocent, spontaneous impulse I have. I will see who I want when I want to, as I have every right to do."

My heart was heavy. I cared deeply for her, but would I give up everything for her? Would I need to, in fact, take her to a desert island in order to keep her out of trouble? It was too much to contemplate. I was not the rebel she was.

"If you are unwilling to conform to some of the basic etiquette of our community, Miss Miller, then I will need some time to contemplate whether or not I am the kind of man you want to associate yourself with."

"There you go being indirect again. Please do me the courtesy of being straightforward. It is not whether *I* want to be with *you* that troubles you, but whether *you* want to be with *me*. Take all the time you need to think it over. Meanwhile, I will be living my life as I see fit."

I left Miss Miller feeling more despondent than I'd ever been in my life. Moving out of her aura was like stepping from warm sun to cold shadow. I actually shivered as I descended the stairs of her apartment building. As I reached the door, Mrs. Miller and Randolph were entering the building and I greeted them with as much warmth as I could muster.

"Mr. Winterbourne," said Randolph, "don't forget that you promised to take me back to the exposition. There is so much more I want to see there!"

"I did promise you that, didn't I? And I will do it, but I don't know how soon I will be seeing you again."

Mrs. Miller looked at me with concern.

"Did you quarrel with my sister again?" said Randolph. "I'll tell her not to be mean to you, so you and I can go back to the exposition soon."

"From your mouth to God's ear, young man."

13

DAISY

It was not easy to watch Mr. Winterbourne depart. Up to this point, he has been willing to defend me, even though disapproving of some of my actions. Is what I did *so* terrible? I know that Americans have a particular reverence for marriage, and I include myself among them, but I challenge anyone to tell me how an innocent walk through the city with a married man somehow threatens his relationship with his wife and, apparently, the entire institution of marriage. Do we trust one another so little? Do we make no allowance for male-female friendship? I wonder if this rigidity stems from the male belief—and perhaps more importantly, the female acceptance of it—that females are good for little more than mating and producing and raising children. No one in our community seems able to comprehend that a man and a woman—at least, a married man and a woman—can be friends who share parts of themselves that have nothing to do with mating and raising children.

The withdrawals of invitations to events in the American community continue to arrive. My social life is diminishing rapidly, and with Mr. Winterbourne gone as well I have very few people to associate with. If my French were better, perhaps I could make a whole new set of friends and let the Americans stew in their own juices. But they are my countrymen, and it saddens me to not be included among them.

Thank God for Alouette, who speaks excellent English—as well as speaking the language of a woman with her own mind.

"They are fools, these Americans, to reject someone as vivacious as you! Let them have their parties, which will simply be duller for your absence. I have read of the Puritans who founded your country, and it appears to me that their spirit lives on. Walking with a married man, indeed! In France this is little cause for notice, much less concern. If people want to have affairs, they will have affairs, but a walk along the Seine is hardly indicative of such a thing."

"But how long can I fight them, Alouette? I'm weary of defending myself just for being myself."

"You can fight them your whole life, my friend—and you must! Women will never have the lives they want if they submit to the pressures of society. We are here to change society, not let society change us. It is hard, lonely work. But that is why we have each other. Women must stand together and force the world to take them as they are, not the way society expects them to be. Stay strong, Daisy!"

I don't want to be strong. I just want to be allowed to be myself. But apparently in order to do that I will have to be strong. It is wearying...

14

WINTERBOURNE

I feel the absence of Miss Miller in my life as a physical pain. My heart is congested and I am constantly weary. It's as if she were some magical source of energy that has been withdrawn from my life. But it is I who have withdrawn from that source. All my friends tell me I had no choice, and perhaps that is true, if I wished to be true to myself. But still it feels like a betrayal. I have chosen an abstraction, society, over a living, breathing, extraordinary human being. But perhaps that is the duty of men, to create and defend the abstractions that bind our society together, our touchstones, the values we will not compromise. Miss Miller refuses to see beyond herself, beyond her own good intentions, to the way her actions affect those practical abstractions that make up our social mores. She wants to be an exception, but the whole point of societal rules is to prevent destructive exceptions. Once exceptions are granted, where do they stop? No, I must stand firm. She must learn how to live within the rules of her society, or people such as her will destroy those rules, and then where will we be?

I lunched with Sargent, expecting that, as a member of one of the leading American families in Paris, he would immediately agree.

"Not on your life, Winterbourne. The rules of society are made to be broken, and broken by people just like Miss Miller. She knows herself and is true to herself. Social customs—mores, you call them, but truly they are nothing more than customs—social customs change, and it is extraordinary people like Miss Miller who change them. What a face that young woman has! What eyes! She can see right through us all."

"She's a rebel is what she is, and more often than not, rebels die trying to change things."

"Ah, but those who succeed transform the world they live in. Will she—and other women like her—succeed and take us all along, or will the dead weight of custom crush her?"

"Must you use a term like 'crush'? It conjures up a horrible image of delicate Miss Miller under the iron weight of one of those elephantine devices in the Gallerie du machines, her blood being squeezed from her body!" I shivered at the thought.

"There was never a revolution without bloodshed, Winterbourne, physical or metaphorical bloodshed. Many people we know would bleed mentally if the customs Miss Miller is undermining were to be done away with. Perhaps that is how I should paint her, as a revolutionary standing on the ramparts! But, alas, that's not my style. It will all come down to her eyes, those piercing eyes. Do you think she would sit for me, now, with all of this going on? I would like to capture her in an attitude of rebellion."

"I'm sure she would value a visitor, under the circumstances, especially someone who is sympathetic to her plight."

"Excellent. Then I shall write her this afternoon. I have no commissions at the moment, so it's a perfect opportunity."

"No need to work gratis, Sargent. I'll commission you to paint her. Whatever may happen between us, I want to be able to gaze on her image at this age for the rest of my life."

"You're a romantic, Winterbourne. I admire that about you."

15

DAISY

When John Sargent wrote me about posing for him, I was not only flattered but giddy at the prospect of having company daily for weeks. I was tired of playing whist with mother and taking Randolph to the park to roll his hoop. I accepted immediately, but also inquired as to who had commissioned him to paint me. He replied that the commissioner wished to remain anonymous, but I surmised it was Mr. Winterbourne, which lightened my heart a bit. Even if he refused to be with me, he clearly still held me dear in some way, as I held him, despite his treatment of me. We were simply different souls, and even if we were never again able to be friends, we would have fond memories of each other—and Mr. Winterbourne would have my portrait.

On his first visit, John, which he insisted I call him because of his youth, brought only his sketch pad. We worked in the small parlor in the back of the apartment, because it had good light and faced north, eliminating the direct glare of the sun. John sketched me in various poses, sitting and standing, and asked me to think about the injustice of my ostracization while I posed. That subject was, of course, never far from my mind, so it was easy, if not pleasant, to focus on it. But John is garrulous, so I was not often alone with my thoughts, although he did focus on the subject at hand.

"I must tell you that Winterbourne is suffering mightily over his decision to stop seeing you, and, having seen you two together, I shouldn't wonder that he is. The man can be an absolute stick sometimes, but with you he seems to come alive. I am convinced that it is your insistence on being your sparkling self that animates him, and, yet, that is what you are being punished for—by him and everyone else."

"It means a great deal to me to hear you say that, John. I had begun to wonder if I had any allies at all in the American community."

"I'm sure there are others too timid to speak out. The world is changing, Miss Miller, and women such as you are leading the way. Others will catch up eventually."

"I'm not trying to lead a revolution. I'm just being myself."

"Which is revolutionary! Do you know how many people spend their lives repressing their true selves in order to be accepted in society. Believe me, I know of what I speak."

"You don't appear to be repressed in any way, John."

"If only you knew. But we're not here to focus on me. You are the subject of the painting, and it is your spirit I wish to capture."

He worked silently for a good while, and the more I thought about what he'd said, the more defiant I became.

"That's it," he said. "That is the look I want to capture. Stay with your thoughts."

Why was society afraid of me? What sort of social damage was everyone afraid I would cause? Why couldn't a woman a little out of the ordinary be tolerated? Society was so dominant that one would think it could absorb variations without collapsing. Yet, people were reacting as if insignificant Daisy Miller had the power to topple the whole edifice. If society were a tree, flexible, able to sway in the breeze, instead of a rigid edifice, it wouldn't be toppled quite so easily. It takes a tornado to uproot a tree, and my little transgressions hardly amounted to that.

"Excellent," said John. "You have given me all I need to work on your face. Now I need to consider what you should be wearing in the portrait."

"Would you like to see my dresses?"

"Oh, no. My subjects rarely have the costume appropriate for my portraits. I have my own ideas, and am not beyond purchasing something new, if it is just right. I have a certain thing in particular in mind. I shall find it and bring it along for our next session. I will decide on the pose as well as the costume by then, and will need to sketch you in the pose I will paint you. I will return in two days."

"You are confident you can do all of that in just two days."

"*Absolument.*"

16

WINTERBOURNE

Sargent is kind enough to bring me word of Miss Miller's state of mind. He said she seems lonely, but is utterly convinced of her innocence. In fact, I believe her intent *was* innocent—and I defend her for that with everyone with whom I discuss the situation in the American community. But she is woefully neglectful of the effects of her actions, or doesn't care about those effects. He also says that she has guessed it was I who commissioned her portrait, and I am glad of that. At least she knows that I retain real affection for her, despite my behavior.

Not long after I spoke with Sargent about her, Miss Miller sent me a brief missive. In it, she put forward her new hypothesis that society should be flexible as a tree, not rigid as an edifice, and I must say that her metaphor affected me. She is right about the rigidity of society, but I have always believed that strength requires rigidity. But when I consider the strength of one of the mighty oaks on my family's estate back home, and the way it sways in a strong wind to avoid being toppled, I must admit that the combination of strength and flexibility appeals to me. It is difficult for me to believe that this naïve young woman could conceive a vision of society superior to that of her, and my, elders, but Sargent says that she is a revolutionary, and rebels are almost inevitably young. Part of me leans toward joining her revolution, but I have never been anything like a revolutionary.

17

DAISY

When I consider the madness of social propriety, I become incensed. I cannot view what Edward Barnes and I did as anything less than natural and innocent. We have known each other since we were young, attending one of the first coeducational secondary schools in the United States together and we were delighted to meet one another again at the Singers' waltz party. Naturally, we wanted to catch up on our lives since then, and I suggested a walk along the Seine. A walk! A perfectly innocent walk in public, among hundreds of promenaders. And now we are treated as if we met clandestinely in a hotel room! I have now learned that it was Mrs.

Barnes, in a jealous fit, who spread the word throughout the American community about my stroll with her husband, and now I am, once again, a pariah. What a ridiculous world we live in! Edward sent a note apologizing for his wife's behavior, but also informing me that it would be imprudent for us to meet again. He apparently suffered no consequences beyond his wife's displeasure, while I was ostracized.

What made it worse was when Mr. Winterbourne appeared at my door, full of good intentions but unable to restrain his natural urge to lecture me on propriety. It was Mrs. Walker disapproving of my actions from her carriage in Rome all over again—and this time Mr. Winterbourne got into the carriage with her!

Today, I sat over my afternoon tea pondering all of this, frustrated at my inability to affect the situation, and trying to ascertain what course of action I might take. Then, I hit upon it. Mrs. Barnes was at the center of it all. It was she I had apparently offended so deeply, and it was she I would be obliged to confront, if I wanted to effect a change. I could just hear Mr. Winterbourne counseling me against this "rash" behavior, but fortunately he was not there to express his disapproval. Knowing I had best strike while the iron was hot, before my courage failed me, I immediately wrote a note to Mrs. Barnes, assuring her of my innocence in regard to her husband and requesting an audience with her to explain my behavior. I knew that the chances of her accepting my offer were slim, but I sealed the note and sent it off by messenger. Why not try? At worst, nothing would change. At best, I would have the opportunity to relieve this woman of her anxiety, making it clear that I had nothing in mind but platonic friendship with her husband.

Just after dinner, I received her reply. I hesitated about opening it, expecting to be excoriated and told never to darken her door. She *was* highly tentative about seeing me, and warned me that she thought me a wanton woman, but I also sensed a curiosity about meeting a creature so willing to flaunt custom, and in the end she invited me for morning coffee at her home the next day. Mother thought I was a fool for walking into what she was certain was an ambush. She was convinced that all Mrs. Barnes wanted to do was give me a dressing-down. But I was willing to chance that. I needed desperately to try to change my situation somehow, even at the risk of making things worse.

The following morning, I put on my most conservative clothing for the occasion and appeared at the Barnes's door promptly at ten o'clock, as requested. The maid let me in, and as I was escorted down the hall, Edward appeared at the far end and gave me a concerned look. I just smiled, trying to reassure him, although I had no idea if my appearance would alter his situation for better or worse. I was let into the drawing room, where Mrs. Barnes sat on a loveseat before a low table that held a blue and white enamel coffee pot and cups on a tray. She did no rise upon my entry, but invited me to sit down without too much rancor in her voice. She was a very pretty blonde—much prettier than I, in my opinion—and wore a pure white dress, perhaps to emphasize her moral superiority.

I sat. She poured coffee and handed it to me without speaking—without, in fact, looking me in the eye, Then she poured her own, and only when she had picked it up and sat back on loveseat she occupied, did her eyes meet mine.

"So," she said. "You are the scarlet woman who has scandalized the entire American community."

"Only with your assistance, Madame. It is you who have made a scandal of a perfectly innocent meeting."

"So my husband says. But, then, that is what you both *would* say to protect your reputations. But it is well-known among the responsible members of society that married men do not attend to single women in unchaperoned situations."

"Indulge me for a moment, Mrs. Barnes, by imagining a world where custom does not cause innocent encounters to be misconstrued as immoral."

"That is not the kind of world in which I care to reside. Rules are rules. They are necessary to preserve the moral fiber of our society."

"What kind of moral fiber does a society have that sees innocence and reads it as immorality? It seems to me that it is *society* that has an impure mind, not myself or your husband, who are nothing but old school friends sharing news after years apart—in full public view, with no attempt at subterfuge. What, pray tell, is immoral about that, except in the jaded eye of 'society'?"

Mrs. Barnes blinked and looked a bit unsure.

"I don't make the rules, Miss Miller."

"But you do, don't you see? Or, at least you preserve them by enforcing them. If you had not reported your husband's supposed transgression to your friends in such negative terms, it would have passed unacknowledged."

"That is where you are wrong, Miss Miller. All eyes are upon us at all times. It was my good friend Emily Stokes—a girl *I* went to secondary school with among other girls, not among boys—who reported seeing you together. Emily would have spread the word herself, so I stole a march on her. I'm not the only one who believes in rules."

"Is that who you call a good friend, someone who is ready to embarrass you the moment she has the opportunity, because your husband broke the almighty rules of society? That is exactly the kind of social pettiness that having so many unnecessary rules engenders."

"Would you have anarchy, then?"

"It is a *long* road from oppressive social norms to anarchy, Mrs. Barnes. I should think we could land somewhere in-between."

Mrs. Barnes sipped her coffee meditatively for some time and then put her cup down before speaking.

"How do you do it?" she asked.

"Do what?"

"So brazenly disregard the rules of society. I would be terrified to act as you do."

"I am only true to myself, Mrs. Barnes. And if that—"

"Call me Jenny, please," she said.

"Very well, Jenny. I can't seem to help being true to my nature. I am not a schemer. If I am interested in talking to someone, I talk to him—or her. Who is to say that I shouldn't be allowed to do that? Why should I have to be clandestine about it? Is that healthier than being straightforward? I think not."

"You are an original, Miss Miller. I've never met anyone like you. I can see why my husband wanted to reacquaint himself with you. That and the fact that you are beautiful."

"Certainly not more beautiful than you. I think it's foolish for anyone to think that your husband would ever choose me over you romantically."

"Now you're acting the *naif*, Miss Miller. No man I've ever known is invulnerable to a *new* pretty face, no matter how pretty the face of the woman he is currently with. And men dare to talk about women being inconstant!"

"Be that as it may, *we* do not need to cooperate with men in their inconstancy, do we? Even if your husband was courting me—which he most assuredly was not—I would not cooperate with his fantasy. I believe men and women can be friends, and if that is some sort of anarchy, then I am indeed an anarchist."

"It was very brave of you to come here today, Miss Miller."

"Daisy, please."

"You are extraordinarily forthright, Daisy. I believe you would be a good friend. Perhaps you and I will be friends, one day."

"I would like that."

"In the meantime, I will call off the dogs, as far as I can. I'm sure you are well aware that once a story is out in society, it is not easy to call back."

"That is precisely why I hate our hidebound society. I was ostracized by the Americans in Rome for friendship with a man and am afraid the same is happening here in Paris."

"I will do what I can to rescue your reputation."

"I appreciate that, Jenny. I had no intention of hurting or upsetting you, and I'm happy that you understand that, now."

"You know, I planned to condemn in you in no uncertain terms today. That is the only reason I invited you here."

"I suspected as much—and my mother was certain of it. I am relieved that we have gotten beyond that."

"Curiously, I am, too."

18

WINTERBOURNE

There is no one like her in the world! Miss Miller's honesty and straightforwardness have triumphed! Jenny Barnes, who one would expect to be her most furious detractor and the one least likely to forgive her, has let it be known that there is nothing between Miss Miller and her husband, and, in fact, has invited Miss Miller to be part of the artistic salon that the Barnes's hold semi-weekly in their home. People who have been angling for an invitation to that exclusive salon for years are out-raged. They—and not a few others in the American community—are convinced that Miss Miller has be-witched Jenny Barnes. But that is true only in the sense that a woman such as Miss Miller—as if there were another woman like her—takes people off guard with her sincerity and her inability to speak an untruth. There is a charm in such behavior that makes her irresistible, and clearly Jenny Barnes could not resist.

Although I applaud and admire Miss Miller, I wonder if she is merely the exception, the person to whom the rules do not apply. How many of us are capable of her spontaneity and candor? How many of us are as guileless? Can an entire society function without the many social rules that hold us together as civilized people? Miss Miller and I have debated this frequently since these recent events unfolded, now that I can safely be with her again. It took some convincing that she should see me again, but she finally allowed it.

"Not everyone is as pure of purpose as you, Miss Miller," I said during one of our discussions.

"It's not a matter of purity of purpose," she replied vehemently. "It's about allowing people to be who they are, about being straightforward, about not hiding behind custom."

"But purity does matter. What about someone who is intent on doing evil things, small or large?"

"Such people won't follow the rules you establish to try to hedge them in, anyway—or they'll follow them only to advance their subterfuge. Your rules are things such people can hide behind, looking proper on the surface and all the time scheming out of sight to take advantage of you. Without so many rules, people can just be themselves—they can *only* be themselves—and if they are wolves, we will see them as wolves. All the petty rules provide is sheep's clothing for them to hide in."

"A pretty metaphor, Miss Miller, but—

"Thank you, Mr. Winterbourne."

"But pretty metaphors don't necessarily capture truth."

"How many times have you read of people who were accepted into the highest social circles, who followed all the customs perfectly to make themselves acceptable, and then turned out to be taking advantage of the people who so enthusiastically approved of them, bilking them of money and property—of daughters even! If those aren't wolves in sheep's clothing, I don't know what else to call them."

But does the fact that people can hide behind social customs make the customs invalid? Miss Miller argues that they bring out the worst in people, instead of the best, that they encourage insincerity and stifle people (with herself in mind, I'm sure) who want only to be sincere and true to themselves. Is she right? Or is she positing an ideal world that will never exist?

Full of renewed affection for Miss Miller, I escorted her to her first salon at the Barnes's home. Her reputation preceded her, of course, and I noticed some women holding tighter to the arms of their husbands or lovers and others who gazed at her with admiration. All of the men admired her, but that has ever been the case. Sargent was there, too, and was the first to greet us.

"Ah, Miss Miller, the triumphant revolutionary! I may reconsider painting you as a victorious revolutionary atop a pile of bodies, like the courageous lady Liberty in Delacroix's *Liberty Leading the People*!"

"Will you require me to expose by breasts, as she does?" asked Miss Miller coolly.

I blushed deeply, but Sargent just laughed.

"I believe you've been in enough trouble without doing something as scandalous as that, my dear. No, I believe we've struck the right tone in our portrait. Has Miss Miller told you about it, Winterbourne?"

"She has not."

"I found a double-breasted woman's coat that hints of a military uniform without being too obvious, and I've posed Miss Miller staring defiantly out a window, her lower body in a pool of light, as if nature herself is supporting her defiance. It is something more in the Vermeer style than anything I've painted before. I believe you will like it, Winterbourne."

"If it's a true portrait of Miss Miller, I know I will."

She just smiled at this statement, as if my affection was her due.

Mrs. Barnes was the next to approach, taking Miss Miller's hand.

"It is good to have you here, Daisy," she said. Then she added drolly, "I believe you've met my husband."

All of us laughed at her risqué humor, which relaxed the atmosphere in the room immediately. I couldn't help admiring Mrs. Barnes's generosity of spirit. I also couldn't help noticing that she called Miss Miller Daisy. I wondered if I would ever be privileged to be on familiar enough terms with Miss Miller to call her by her first name. After the recent unpleasantness between us, I imagined it might be some time before she allowed that —which was as it should be. I had to earn back her trust.

The salon was most entertaining. Not being a literary sort, myself, I had never been to such an event, and I was impressed by the poets, novelists, and musicians who performed. Expecting to be somewhat bored, I found myself fully engaged for the entire evening. Miss Miller's eyes were glowing at the end, and she went immediately to thank Mrs. Barnes for including her the evening.

"Perhaps I'll ask you to lecture us on the stricture of social customs at the next salon, my dear," said Mrs. Barnes.

Miss Miller turned pale.

"I'm just having a bit of fun with you, Daisy," she reassured her.

"Perhaps one of the fine writers here tonight will take up the subject," said Miss Miller.

"You may have noted that they were all men, so I find it unlikely. We are woefully lacking in female writers. Did you ever consider writing, yourself, Daisy?"

"I never have, but I feel inspired tonight, so perhaps one day..."

"I encourage you to give it a try. You have a clear mind, deep human sympathy, and a perspective on women and society we all need to hear. We have Jane Austen and George Eliot and America's own Louisa May Alcott, but a fresh American female voice would be most welcome."

"What a nice thing to say, Jenny."

"Coffee on Monday at ten?"

"I look forward to it."

As I helped Miss Miller on with her coat, I said, "You've made a conquest! Jenny Barnes has never been easy for anyone to get close to, but she seems to relish your friendship."

"And I hers. We survived great adversity together and that has brought us close."

"You have beaten your swords into ploughshares, you two—enemies turned into friends. It's a fine example of magnanimity for all of us."

19

DAISY

It is a strange "activity" sitting for a portrait. One feels honored and alternately egotistical and unworthy having an artist focusing on one exclusively. John talks much less, now that he is actually applying paint to canvas, so there is much room—perhaps too much room—for my thoughts to wander. I have been thinking about Jenny's suggestion that I try writing. It was flattering, but I have no idea if I have the talent to actually write something— to put paint to canvas, as it were. I'm an avid reader, but I fear that the leap between *reading* good books and *writing* them is across a great chasm. Perhaps I will try a few sketches of ideas and characters to see if I have any aptitude. I may be too social to apply myself with pen and paper for hours on end, although my recent forced isolation has shown me that I can maintain myself in solitude when I need to.

I also cannot help worrying about when I will next violate the boundaries of propriety just by being myself. Though my ostracism was brief, I felt its sting in a way I never have before. Am I becoming less courageous about being who I am, whatever the consequences? I pray I am not, because nothing is more important to me than the honest expression of myself. Before all of this—perhaps beginning with the snubs by Mrs. Walker and Mrs. Costello in Rome—it had never even occurred to me that just being who I am could offend people so deeply. It makes me wonder sometimes why God made me this way, instead of docile and contented with doing things according to custom. But God *did* make me this way, so who am I to try to be someone else? Perhaps I need to pray more to my Creator for support in being the person I was made. I would like to use this argument with those who accuse me of being perverse, but they would only insist that Satan was behind my way of being, not God—and I *know* that's not true! I may be many things, but evil is not one of them. So I can only go with God.

I want very much to see how my portrait is progressing, but John will not hear of it. Perhaps he is a bit insecure himself, so doesn't want to show his work until he thinks it's perfect. Of course, I could peek. The canvas is too large for him to take away with him every day, so it stands covered on its easel in the parlor. But I am an honorable woman (despite what others may say), so I will respect his wishes. But sometimes it takes all of the will power I possess to resist looking!

20

WINTERBOURNE

I am back in Miss Miller's good graces. It took some weeks, but she has finally forgiven me fully for my reaction to her indiscretion. She established this symbolically by giving me permission to call her Daisy, so farewell Miss Miller and hello sweet Daisy! It really does feel much more intimate to use her Christian name—not that there is any St. Daisy she was named after (which somehow seems appropriate, in her case), but it *is* what her family and close friends call her. So, now I can count myself a close friend, if not family—but perhaps someday... Daisy Winterbourne has a fine ring to my ear. That is, when it does not strike fear into my heart. To be joined with such a woman would be like joining a revolution, and I am not certain I'm up to that. So, until I have the courage—if I ever do—to ask her to marry me, she will just be my good friend Daisy.

And perhaps that is how it should remain. Daisy continues to cause me discomfort in social situations, putting herself out to people she hardly knows as if they were intimates. She seems to have no discrimination about who she spends time with; the only test is whether a person is interesting to her. If they are, she takes an interest. Whether it's a street sweeper or a famous author makes no difference to her. She treats all as equals. I realize that this is the American ideal, but, really, an ideal is something to aim for, not something to put into practice on the street every day. I'm sorry, but all men are *not* created equal. Or, they may be *created* equal, but circumstances of class and education and refinement quickly make some human beings superior. It seems unrealistic not to recognize this.

And she doesn't recognize superior people any better than inferior ones. She talks with people above her station or older and more experienced or famous for great achievement as frankly as she talks to the street sweeper. She once asked a princess about her sleeping habits, told the mayor of Paris about her drinking too much at a party, and asked a great author to write a little story about her—and I'll be damned if the man didn't do it!

Is it possible to live with a woman who continually embarrasses you? Is it possible to get over being embarrassed by such a woman? These are the questions I must answer to my satisfaction before I can get any more serious about Daisy.

And then, of course, there is biggest question: Would she even accept my proposal?

21
DAISY

John finished my portrait and invited my mother and Frederick—Mr. Winterbourne and I are on a first-name basis, now—to view the unveiling. Randolph was invited, too, but had no interest. (The boy is much more likely to become an athlete and eventually take over the family business than to be an artist of any sort.) John seemed eager to share the painting, so he must be happy with it. We assembled in the salon, and John gave a little introductory speech before removing the cloth that covered the canvas.

"It has been a joy to work with you, Daisy. You are a magnificent subject."

I couldn't help blushing at this.

"You have been most cooperative with my demands and manipulations as I worked on the portrait. The result is a piece I am very proud of. My hope is that it captures both your charm and your determination to be who you really are, not the person society expects you to be. I had originally conceived an image of you looking out a window with a determined look on your face, but then I realized that the viewer would see only one of your magnificent eyes, and that looking away, instead of at the viewer. But I wanted that gaze straight on, challenging the viewer. So, I kept you at the window, but turned your head to the side, as if someone had just entered the room and caught you in a reverie of determination, if that is not a contradiction in terms. That said, I give you: a portrait of Daisy Miller.

John removed the cloth and everyone gasped. It was me, to the life, with an expression that was somehow both challenging and charming. Was I really capable of such an expression or had he invented it? I hoped it was real, because that is how I think of myself, determined to be who am (which is charming, if I do say so myself) and also determined to ward off anyone who would attempt to prevent me from being myself. The double-breasted, almost military black coat hung open, exposing just the top curve of one pink-white breast. My hair was loose, almost as if I'd just come into the house and it was still wind-blown. The sun was high in the sky, therefore creating a pool of light at my feet on the light carpet, which gave my figure an almost angelic quality, as if I were standing on a sunlit cloud. The image forced the viewer to ask if this woman is like a soldier, an angel, a coquette, or somehow a combination of all three. I had never before considered my own complexity, but John's painting compelled me to do that. I felt both proud and confused about who I was, as represented here.

Frederick was the first to speak.

"You have outdone yourself, John. It's breathtaking. It captures Miss Miller's—Daisy's—fascinating and complicated personality—not to mention her extraordinary beauty—perfectly. I told you I wanted an image that would allow me to remember her as she is now for the rest of my life, and you have done that. Amazing. I will be eternally grateful to you."

"You look a bit frightening to me, dear," said Mrs. Miller. "But, then, you do scare me sometimes, so I suppose that's appropriate."

"You've not spoken, yet, Daisy," said John. "Are spellbound or appalled or somewhere in-between?"

"I love it!" I exclaimed. "Am I really that interesting, because I find myself very interested in this young woman?"

John and Frederick smiled at one another.

"I believe that Frederick will agree with me that, in fact, you are endlessly fascinating."

"Hear, hear," said Frederick.

"You will allow me to visit myself, sometimes, won't you Frederick?"

"You know that you are always welcome in my home—properly chaperoned, of course," he said, looking at my mother, who just shrugged.

It was impossible to look at this image and not like myself. And that was a wonderful feeling, after all I'd been through.

22

WINTERBOURNE

Is it possible for a man to fall more deeply in love with a woman just by gazing at a portrait of her? That is what seemed to happen, once the painting of Daisy was installed in my study. Every day, I would sit in front of it, with coffee in the morning, with tea in the afternoon, with a glass of port in the evening, and marvel at how fascinating this young woman was. But I wanted more than a painting of her. I wanted her to be my wife—or imagined I did. The thought of this magnificent woman being part of my daily life was almost overwhelming—and, yes, there was an element of fear in that thought as well as attraction.

For better or worse, then, John Sargent, who had

created this spellbinding image of the woman I dreamed of marrying, also delivered the *coup de grâce* to my immediate hopes of winning Daisy, by introducing her to a young American painter who had studied with him at the Ecole des Beaux-Arts. Anton Leclerc was, it must be said, one of the handsomest men I have ever seen. But Daisy has never been one to have her head turned by a pretty face alone—although she was hardly immune to such attraction—but Leclerc was also intelligent, sophisticated, charming, and, if he was to be believed, an advocate of women's rights in all spheres of life. His French parents had taken the family to live New York City for a time when he was teenager, so he had developed both continental *savoir faire* and American straightforwardness. He was also the same age as Daisy, and while I was only five years older, five years is five years. Daisy was aware that her attraction to Anton was painful for me, but said, "You had your chance, Frederick. We were growing closer when you chose society over me in the Barnes affair. Although I have accepted you back as a good friend, you dimmed my romantic feelings for you. One wants to be loved unconditionally, not just when she is on her best behavior."

And so I watched them, she and Leclerc, out and about at all the American parties, saw everyone admiring their beauty, grace, and charm, the way the seemed to fit together. Because of his family, he had French connections, too, of course, and I'm sure they were equally admired at French parties. Leclerc knew of my attraction to Daisy, knew I'd had her portrait painted, and liked to josh me about it.

"I hear you had a chance with Daisy, yourself, once,"

he said. "Pity you didn't take advantage of the opportunity. My good luck, I guess"

When she brought him to my home to show him Sargent's painting, he said, "She's so much more wonderful in person than in oils, Winterbourne!"

I am tempted to punch him every time he makes such comments, but civilization prevails. Perhaps I should punch him, demonstrating to Daisy how much I care. No doubt she would just resent me for spoiling his pretty face.

The one saving grace in the situation is that Daisy really seems to be in love with him, to be happy in his company, and since I love her—and also wonder if I could ever have made her happy, or been completely happy with her—there is some satisfaction in that. At least she is with just *one* man, now, most of the time, and Leclerc doesn't seem to mind her casual interactions with other men as I had. Perhaps he is the kind of progressive man she needs.

23

DAISY

Anton was a revelation to me. First, his beauty, which all women seem to find breathtaking—and men threatening. I can't deny there was a stirring in my body when I first saw him. And he tells me that he had a similar response to me—to my surprise, frankly. I know I am attractive, but never thought of myself as turning men's heads the way Anton turns women's. But Frederick assures me that I am wrong, that men have always responded to me the same way women respond to Anton. Perhaps we are a good physical match, then. Mother keeps rushing things ahead and talking about how beautiful our children would be.

But the connection of heart and soul is of much more importance to me than a physical connection. The body wilts eventually, but the heart, however weakened, continues to love, and the soul is ageless. It is the heart and soul connection that lasts a lifetime. And I feel that with Anton. He takes me as I am, encourages my independence, supports my belief in the rights of women. He is also an artist, and he looks at the world with the appreciative eye of an artist. I have always taken great joy in the physical world, and he does the same. He sees values far beyond money—a prerogative of the well-off, I know, but there you have it. And he is an advocate for the rights of women, something very few men are today.

"It's ridiculous, Daisy," he said once. "Any honest man who has known an intelligent woman must admit that there is no difference between *his* intelligence and *hers*. What does the configuration of the body have to do with the functioning of the mind? And an equally ridiculous argument is that there are no great female artists, when men have never *allowed* women to fully express their creativity. Look at Mary Cassatt, our own American expatriate. Now that women are being allowed to exercise their full creative powers as men always have, society is producing artists like her right out of the gate, doing work as good as any of the male Impressionists. And the same is true of writers like Austen and Eliot and Alcott. Who needs more evidence that it was only the *repression* of women's talent that prevented them from creating work that matches that of men?"

It thrills me when Anton says such things. And he doesn't just say them to please me. He makes the same arguments in social situations where men make light of the idea of equality for women. The older men write him off as an ignorant youth, but he doesn't care, even though some of those men are potential patrons of his work and might reject him for his "radical" ideas. I admire his speaking out without weighing the cost.

I love being alone with him, too, although I'm sure society would be scandalized by my doing so without a chaperone. I love to sit with Anton in his studio while he works, and there is no danger of anything untoward happening between us there, because his concentration on his work is absolute. I believe I could disrobe and he would not notice! So, I sit and read or do needlepoint, and lately I have begun scratching a few lines on paper, testing out my capacity for writing—with little success, so far. Frederick insists that mediocrity is a starting place and that I must be patient, but patience has never been my foremost virtue. Anton's work inspires me, but his painting is so much more advanced than my writing that it also makes me feel inferior.

If Anton has a shortcoming, it is his inability to relate to my little brother Randolph. Anton is also a youngest child, and I fear that two them do not mix well. Both expect to be the center of attention. Anton has had little experience with children as an adult, and can't seem to access the young boy in himself, so he is awkward and uncomfortable with Randolph. My brother did not endear himself any further to Anton when he said the other day, in Anton's presence, "Where's Frederick? I like Frederick better than this man." Frederick is kind enough to continue spending time with Randolph. He recently took him back to the Exposition Universelle, which Randolph had been harping on for months. Frederick is a good man and a good friend.

24

WINTERBOURNE

It still pains me deeply to see Daisy with Leclerc, but I am working my way toward acceptance of the situation. I have come to realize that, even if she and I are never together as husband and wife, I still want to be her friend, enjoy her company—which has delighted me since the moment I met her in Vevey. And Leclerc is not such a bad sort. Sometimes I feel that his speeches on women's rights are as much for show as anything else, a way to set himself apart from the normal run of artists and intellectuals as a revolutionary, and to endear himself to Daisy. But he makes good arguments, and he is capable of discussing subjects such art and history and politics with intelligence and insight. I enjoy conversing with him. He is a bit full of himself for my taste, but it's not as if he neglects Daisy to win attention for himself. He listens when she speaks and seems to respect what she says. And, to my surprise, the three of us get on quite well. Some people look askance at Daisy on the arms of two men, but perhaps I am becoming more like her, because I don't care. We all know that our being together is innocent, so damn the filthy minded!

We had our most intense interaction after attending a radical play performed by a company called Women With Wings, which was founded by a small group of American feminist expatriates. Daisy's friend Aloutte had introduced her to Hubertine Auclert, a strong-minded French feminist and founder of the women's suffrage movement in France, and Mademoiselle Auclert had recommended the company's most recent play, *A Woman Exits*. None of us knew the plot, but it turned out to be about a woman who not only leaves her husband, but also her children, when she realizes that life as a wife and mother is stifling her. Her husband is not unfaithful or abusive to her; it is simply that her life is constrained to a point where she feels trapped in her roles as wife and mother. (It turned out that this plot had been "imported" by one of the actresses, who had seen a performance of *A Doll's House* in Norway.)

We went to a matinee, and afterward ate supper together at a restaurant near the theatre. Over champagne and good food, we argued the morality of what the main character had done.

"But what had the husband done," I asked, "to be treated so cavalierly?"

"It's not *about* the husband," Daisy retorted. "Men

always want it to be about them. It was something *she* had to do—not *against* husband but *for* herself."

"So, you *approve* of such behavior?"

"I don't know. It's hard to imagine myself in that situation. But it was right for her."

"It's not as if it's a real situation, Winterbourne," said Leclerc. "It's a play making a point about women feeling trapped by the limits of the only roles society considers acceptable for them."

"But it also suggests a solution: abandonment of one's family! It's abhorrent."

"Don't be so literal, my friend," he replied. "It's about women as a whole throwing off their traditional roles and limitations. It's saying they can be more than they've been if they break free."

"I hadn't thought of it that way," said Daisy, "but I think Anton is right. It's a message about men and women as part of society, not just in one individual situation."

"It's fine to go on about symbolism, but how many women not acquainted with that symbolic level of meaning are going to take it literally and think they should abandon their families? I think it's irresponsible."

"So, you're saying that women are too simpleminded to get the symbolism?" said Daisy.

"No! You said yourself that you hadn't thought about it as symbolic until Anton pointed it out. But not all women—or men, for that matter—think on that level. They see performers on stage acting out what appears to be a semblance of a real life, and they think of it as a story about real life, not as an allegory."

"He makes a good point, Daisy. It only occurred to

me while we were sitting here that the playwright was being symbolic. Until that moment, I had been considering what I would think if something of that sort happened in real life."

"Then perhaps we need to take up that subject," said Daisy.

"That ought to liven up the discussion!" said Leclerc.

"Do either of you really dare to justify what that woman did?" I said.

"I do," said Daisy. "You can't know the pain of being held back, day after day, month after month, year after year, the way a woman can, Frederick. For a woman with a free spirit, like the character in the play, it can lead to madness."

"Well, that much is clear," I said. "What she did was certainly mad!"

"In your opinion," said Daisy.

"In the opinion of any sane person in society!"

"Are you calling *me* insane?"

"If the shoe fits..."

"Let me jump in here, before you two come to blows," said Leclerc. "Obviously, her leaving her husband isn't *so* unusual. Society doesn't *like* divorce, but it a happens a good deal in spite of the that. I'm sure it's her leaving her children that you find morally abhorrent, Winterbourne. Am I right?"

"I don't like either action, but, yes, it's the abandoning of her children that sticks in my craw."

"Can you imagine someone of Daisy's sensitivity doing something like that?"

"No, I can't."

"Then perhaps we can stop making this personal."

"Perhaps you two gentlemen should ask *me*," said Daisy, "if I think I could do something like that, not decide *for me* that I'm too sensitive to ever consider it."

"Well," I said, "could you?"

"I believe things would have to be worse than they were for the woman in the play, but, yes, if the need to get away were strong enough, I can imagine doing it. I've never had children, so I can't really imagine the cost of leaving them, but I *do* know that I'm tired of men assuming that the care of children is *only* the responsibility of women. So many men seem to think that if they earn a living for the family, their responsibility ends there. The husband in the play will clearly need help with his children, since he has a job, but there is no reason in the world why he can't take on the emotional responsibility for raising them."

"I'm not sure that men are equipped to do that," said Lelerc.

"Then they *need* to equip themselves," said Daisy. "The world is going to change, and those who don't change with it will be adrift."

"Is that a line from one of your feminist pamphlets?" I asked, with a scornful tone that I immediately realized was unnecessary.

"As a matter of fact, it is my own original thought. I have them, you know."

"I'm sorry, Daisy. Heat of the moment and all that. I am well aware that you have a most original mind."

"Apology accepted."

25

DAISY

Next to meeting Anton, nothing has enlivened my life recently more than Alouette introducing me to Hubertine Auclert. We were to meet over tea at Alouette's apartment, and I asked if I could bring Jenny Barnes along with me. Jenny is waking up to feminism, after realizing that her reaction to my walk with her husband said more about her than about me or her husband. Feeling trapped and limited by her roles, she had felt threatened by a young woman who clearly wasn't so bound by societal strictures.

Hubertine—and she insisted immediately that we call her that, saying that "sisters" ought to call each other by their given names—is an extraordinary woman. In addition to leading the women's suffrage movement in France, she is in the planning stages of a feminist journal that will take on the issues women face in their drive for equality in daily life. It occurred to me immediately that, if I became serious about writing, her magazine might be an outlet for my work—although it felt as if I were a long way from producing anything of that length or quality. But one must have something to strive for.

I had thought that Hubertine might be one of those social leaders who can talk of nothing but the issues that concern them, but she took in Jenny and me as individuals (she already knew Aloutte fairly well), asking us about lives and our reasons for being drawn to the movement. She was particularly taken with my story, because my attraction to the movement had grown not out of some dramatic experience—abuse by a man, being stymied in a profession, being exhausted from doing nothing but raise children—but simply from realizing that because I was a woman I was not allowed to be my unconventional, outgoing self.

"This is what our movement is about at its core," said Hubertine. "Men are allowed such a wide range of behavior, so much more freedom, whereas we are expected to limit ourselves in education, work, social life, politics, and so on. We won't necessarily *want* some of the things men have, *do* some of the things they do, but we should be allowed to *consider* them, just as a man would: to socialize with whoever we want; to be unmarried and not be ridiculed because of it; to win a Ph.D. in any area of study that interests us; and, for that matter, to become a stevedore and load ships, if we have the physical strength to do it. Men most often do what they want to do; women most often do what they're expected to do, allowed to do."

It was refreshing to me to be told that being who I wanted to be was normal, not an aberration. And I could see that this concept was lighting up Jenny, too.

"I've always wanted to be a writer," she blurted out after Hubertine's little speech. "But my husband says it's ridiculous, that I have enough to do raising our children and keeping house. I love my children—in fact, I want to write stories for children—but I'm more than a wife and mother. He needs to see that. I need time to pursue my own interests. He goes to his club and to the races, he sings in a men's choir at our church, he carves chess sets as gifts for friends, just because he loves doing those things. I want to be able to do something just because I love doing it."

"And you shall," said Hubertine. "You might be surprised at how easy it is to get what you want, once you realize what it is and have the courage to demand it. Is your husband a reasonable man?"

"Yes, he is."

"Then you may be one of the lucky ones. Some men hold their wives down almost for sport, because they think they can—and, of course, law and custom support that attitude. But the more small battles we can win, like yours and like Daisy's battle with oppressive social norms, the easier it will be to start changing things on a larger scale."

I thought back to how lonely I'd felt when I was ostracized for my innocent walk with Edward Barnes, and realized that it would have been so much easier to bear if I'd had a coterie of women I could trust and talk with about what had happened, women who would understand and sympathize. I decided then and there that I would ask Aloutte and Jenny to form such a group, with ourselves as the core, inviting others as we found more kindred spirits.

Jenny and I also volunteered when Hubertine told us she needed help planning and organizing a women's suffrage march through Paris that was scheduled for mid-autumn. It was good to take control of conditions in our individual lives, but if grander changes were going to happen, laws needed to change, and laws were made by elected politicians, politicians elected by voters, who were exclusively male.

A few days after this meeting, I received a note from Jenny saying that she'd confronted Edward about having time to write and he'd been supportive of the idea. He'd been less enthusiastic about her becoming involved with the women's suffrage movement, but she had insisted and he had come around grudgingly. I wrote back congratulating her and suggesting that, since we both wanted to write, we do it together.

Poor mother is bewildered by my becoming "political," as she calls it, all of a sudden.

"You used to be a girl who just wanted to have a good time, and now you're getting so serious about everything," she says.

"It was society trying to *prevent* me from having a good time that made me serious about the women's movement, Mama. Don't you want to do what you want to do, when you want to do it?"

"Oh, you know me, dear. I want to do as little as possible."

26

WINTERBOURNE

Throughout the fall, I enjoyed socializing with Daisy and Leclerc, and sometimes Edward and Jenny Barnes joined us, even hosting dinner parties for us at their home. We took full advantage of the arts in Paris—music, plays, art exhibitions—and went out into the countryside on warmer days. It was a good life. I had also started seeing two women who interested me, knowing that I had to move on from Daisy and live my own life, and one of them would sometimes accompany us on our outings.

It was one of these women, Marie Chaisson, who told me something shocking. We had left the others behind at a picnic to walk a path through the woods, and as soon as we were out of earshot, she started giggling. I asked her what was so funny.

"It's your friend Daisy," she said. "Does she know anything about Anton Leclerc?"

"She knows he's a painter and an unmarried man. Is there something else she should know?"

"Perhaps that he has an insatiable sexual appetite and acts on it."

I was stunned.

"But he's a friend of John Sargent, and John cares for Daisy. I don't believe he'd introduce her to a man like that."

"He probably doesn't know. Few people do. Apparently Leclerc travels to Marseille regularly to satisfy his appetites."

Daisy had told me that Leclerc traveled regularly to Marseille to see his family, but she had never been invited along. The story Leclerc told her was that he didn't like his family and didn't want to inflict them on her.

"He also sees prostitute—very discreetly on the outskirts of Paris, so none of his city acquaintances will know about his activities."

"If he's so discreet, how do *you* know about it—how do you even know it's *true*?"

"I have a friend who fell on hard times a while back and took up the oldest profession for a time in the area he frequented in Paris. She was very indiscreet. When we drank wine together, she would always have too much and start telling me stories about her clients—by name. I had already met Leclerc at a few parties—in fact, he was briefly interested in me, but I didn't like him—so when my friend started telling me about him, I listened closely. I won't be as indiscreet as she was and relate the details of what he demanded of her, but she did say that he bragged about the willingness of the whores in Marseille to do anything, in order to encourage her to let him do what he wanted with her."

I felt as if my head was spinning, trying to reconcile the Leclerc I knew, that Daisy knew, with the libertine Marie described.

"But he's an advocate of women's rights!" I blurted out, as if that had anything to do with a man's sexual appetites.

"I'm sure he is—the right of women to...do whatever he wants them to do for him in bed!"

I was so shocked I was speechless. Was Marie lying? Why would she lie about such a thing? Perhaps Leclerc had done something to her and she wanted revenge. I had to corroborate her story.

"Would you be willing to take me to your friend as soon as we get back to Paris? I need her to confirm all of this. It beggars belief."

"I'd be happy to. She's not a whore any longer, but she *is* chronically short of money, so if you were willing to pay for the information, she would speak with you."

"Because of the serious nature of this accusation, and because I hardly know you, I must insist that we go to her as soon as we return and that you allow me to ask all the questions."

"I understand. You're worried about your friend—and you should be. Leclerc is not a man I would advise anyone to get serious about."

That very evening, Marie took me to her friend Jeanette's modest apartment. She assured Jeanette that

I was an honest man, who just wanted information on one of her former clients to help a friend, and told her I was willing to pay for the information. Jeanette assented. In order to ensure that Jeanette wouldn't just spin a tale along the lines of what I indicated I wanted to hear, I simply said, "Tell me everything you know about Anton Leclerc." The story she told matched what Marie had told me. So, apparently it was true. Jeanette dashed my final hope—that Leclerc may have done this in the past, but had reformed himself—when she added, unbidden, that her friends still in the business continued to see Leclerc quite often.

I spent a sleepless night with this incendiary information on my mind. I was heartbroken for Daisy, who loved and trusted this man. What I couldn't decide was how to handle the situation. Did I tell Daisy and have her confront Leclerc? Did I tell Leclerc and insist that he discreetly end the relationship with Daisy? Would it be cruel to tell her the truth, or would it be crueler to not tell her and have Leclerc leave her on some false pretext? As dawn came, I decided that it would be patronizing not to tell Daisy the truth and let her make her own decision about the man. It was not a conversation I relished having.

27

DAISY

The planning for suffrage demonstration continues apace. We were originally denied access to the Champs-Élysées, because officials assumed the demonstration would be very small, but we have asked participants to make a reservation if they plan to participate, and we have nearly a two thousand committed to appear. We have requested everyone who is coming to ask friends to participate, so the number continues to grow.

I feel so much less alone, now. Jenny, Alouette, and I have been meeting regularly, sharing experiences of not being seen by men when we want to be seen and being called out for silly things that men have decided women "just don't do." We are all tired of "gentleman" telling us what to do and thinking they know what is best for us. I have come to realize that I've grown tired of transgressing social customs simply by doing things that come naturally to me. I want the autonomy that men have and see no reason why I shouldn't have it. Perhaps human nature can't be changed, but social customs are invented and can be changed any time society is willing to change them, and we aim to encourage those changes.

I continued to enjoy Anton's company, and he mine. I wonder if a proposal is in the offing, but I am certainly in no rush. I have begun to question the wisdom of women marrying in a world where marriage as it is currently defined robs them of their power. Were I to marry, I would like a contract that stipulates what my rights are—which may or may not be legally binding, but it would at least be a basis for divorce if my husband did not live up the terms of the contract. Hubertine is excited about this idea, because such contracts would at least provide a basis for women to establish their rights within a marriage. A man unwilling to grant his wife a reasonable level of autonomy would be exposed if he refused to sign such a contract.

Not that I have any concern about this with Anton. He supports my women's rights activities and has already made a reservation for the march, one of a very small number of men willing to risk the ridicule of their fellows by supporting us publicly. Even Frederick is holding back, not entirely convinced that women should be, as he puts it, "dragged into the sordid business of politics." I think he is also fearful of being made to appear foolish among his fellows for supporting what many men consider a ridiculous cause.

But Anton and I will be there, although not hand-in-hand, as I would prefer, because men are being relegated to the end of the parade, a kind of exclamation point of support demonstrating that women have too long been made to follow men.

28

WINTERBOURNE

In the event, getting myself to initiate the conversation with Daisy about Leclerc was even more difficult than I had anticipated. To discuss with a woman such behavior by any man was most embarrassing, but to discuss it as the behavior of the man she loved would be excruciating. I went to her apartment to have the conversation, so she would at least be on familiar ground when this bombshell exploded. The maid greeted me at the door, and Mrs. Miller appeared first, saying Daisy would be along momentarily. I asked if Daisy and I be could alone in the small parlor in back, the one where Sargent had painted Daisy, and Mrs. Miller agreed, seeing by my demeanor that I had something important to discuss. She left me in the parlor to await Daisy.

I was in such an awful state of anticipation that I nearly felt sick. Finally, Daisy entered. She started to banter immediately, as she is wont to do with me, but then she saw the look on my face and stopped abruptly.

"What is it, Frederick?"

I requested that she sit, and then took a seat directly across from her. I would have been more comfortable standing behind her to reveal such disturbing information, but determined that this would be cowardly.

"This is going to be a most difficult conversation, Daisy, and if there were any better way to get you the information I possess, I would have chosen it. But my affection and concern for you demand that I speak to you in person."

"Good heavens, Frederick, did you murder someone?"

"No. But I feel as if I am about to."

"Whatever can you mean?"

"It was been revealed to me that Anton Leclerc is a libertine, that he has been keeping the company of prostitutes both here and in Marseille for many years."

"My Anton? Why surely that is absurd."

"That was my first reaction, also. I have come to like the man, and I was thunderstruck that he could live such a life. But whatever you and I may think, it is true. He has a dark side to him that he has not revealed to either of us—or apparently to Sargent."

Daisy stood up and started pacing the room. I decided to stay sitting to act as an anchor.

"Surely this is a tale from his past. He is not so long out of art school and we have all heard stories about the wanton lives of art students in Paris. Surely he has thrown over such behavior by now."

"I had the same hope, but it appears that his... activities...continue to this day. Some of the worst of it occurs on his trips to Marseille. In fact, he has no family there and this activity is the sole purpose of his trips."

"So, you are saying that not only has he been acting the wanton, but he has been lying to me about his family as well?"

"I'm sure you understand that he couldn't tell you the *true* purpose of his travels there."

"This is... I don't know what it is... It certainly beggars belief. Frederick, assure me that this is not a pathetic attempt on your part to separate me from Anton."

"Under normal circumstances I would find that question deeply insulting, Daisy, but I know you have had a shock, so I will disregard it. I reveal this information only for your protection, because it appears to me that Anton's behavior would not change even were he to marry you. There are countless married men who conduct their lives this way, and, from what I've been told, Anton's addiction to such activities is stronger than most."

"Who told you this, Frederick? I must know."

"I cannot reveal that, but I assure you that the source is unimpeachable. I will only say that it is a woman who has actually engaged in these activities with Anton in Paris and was told directly by him of his trips to Marseille."

The color had drained from Daisy's face. She look ill.

"I must..." she muttered. "I must...speak to him. I must hear it from his own mouth."

"He may choose to deny it."

"Still. I must confront him. I do not believe he will lie to me when I confront him with the facts."

"But, Daisy, he has been lying to you for months."

"I see that!" she said angrily. "Of course I see that! But I believe I can get the truth out of him. He must admit the truth, now that I know. He must. I will insist upon it."

29

DAISY

I should have been grateful to Frederick for revealing what kind of a man Anton is, but in the moment I hated him for it. He exploded my life. Being with Anton was pleasant and joyful—satisfying in so many ways. And now that life is gone—poof—like a disappearing act in some perverse magic show. Anton a soulless wanton, using women for his pleasure without regard for who they are as human beings. I had, of course, known that some men did this, but to find out that the man I love is one of them is devastating. Was everything about him a lie?

That is what I had to discover, and that is why I went to his studio unannounced, determined to confront him. And with a perverse kind of logic, my doing that is what confirmed without a doubt that he was living a whole separate life from the one he shared with me. His land-lady let me in, knowing I was a frequent visitor, but what she did not reveal to me was that I was not Anton's first visitor that morning. When I opened the door to his studio, he had a naked woman—perhaps one of his models; I don't know and I don't care—backed up against a wall and his pants were down. They were so deeply engaged in their "activity" that they didn't even see me, even though I stood there dumbfounded for a long moment. Then I quietly closed the door and walked away, heartbroken.

I went home and wrote Anton a letter:

My former dearest,

I came to your studio this morning, planning to speak to you about something I'd heard about the way you live your life. I could hardly believe what I'd been told, but when I opened your door and discovered you *in flagrante delicto* with an unknown woman—yes, I was there, but neither of you saw me —I knew that everything I had been told about you was true. Equal to my abhorrence of the way you live your life is my incredulousness about your lying to me. No love relationship can be based on lies—or, for that matter, on indiscriminate wanton-ness. Please do not write to me or attempt to see me. It is over.

With my heart broken,
Daisy

Writing the letter emptied me out. My body felt hollow. I who had played so lightly at life was suddenly heavy of heart. I told mother I was going to bed, and I stayed there through the night and into the morning, and through another day. And then I woke up, and it was as if everything was new. I would live without the man I thought I loved, because he had never truly been that man. I would be me. And that was all I needed.

30

WINTERBOURNE

Daisy suffered over the next few weeks, and to distract herself she threw her energy into the planning of the women's suffrage march, which continued to grow until there were several thousand participants. I still had my doubts about women voting—it just didn't seem to match their nature—but I admired Daisy's dedication, and she kept trying to convince me, trying to make me see that it made no sense for women to be less than full citizens of any country. And as the event approached, I found myself a bit more open to the idea. I hadn't planned on going to the march, but then I thought I should at least be there to demonstrate to Daisy that I cared about something she had put so much effort into.

It was an exciting event. A powerful energy emanated from the mass of females gathered there. They were excited and happy and determined to make an impression on the city. There were signs and banners and French flags and a band playing. Thousands were gathered along the path of the march, some to support the women and many more to scoff and jeer. I stood on the curb at the starting point.

Daisy was walking about telling people how to line up, and when to put their signs up, and what time the march would start. And as I watched her, I had an epiphany. In that moment, in that place, I finally understood what feminism was all about. It was about extraordinary women like Daisy being allowed to display how extraordinary they were. It was about women like her being able to be the lively, open, natural human beings they were, without being held back or constricted. It was about women having the same freedom of movement, of choice, of profession, of activity that men accord themselves. Women are different from men, yes, but it is not a difference in value. What women are is as equally valuable as what men are. We men tend to patronize and infantilize women, but that is only because we refuse to see them as they truly were, refuse to see that equal value. It is shortsighted, ignorant, and oppressive, and it diminishes us as well as them, diminishes our society, because we lose the full value of half our citizens.

And in that moment I also knew without a doubt that I loved Daisy Miller and admired her—that, if I was honest, I had loved and admired her since the first time I had met her, because I sensed that she had things to teach me, things that as a man I couldn't see. And I saw that I didn't want a partner in life who I could control and care for as if she were a child. I wanted a free-thinking adult partner who would challenge me and make me a better man.

When the march started, I waved to Daisy, who looked as happy as I'd ever seen her. I watched wave after wave of strong, determined women go by. And when the dozen or two men who were part of the march came by at the end, I stepped off the curb and joined them.

—END—

Also by Lawrence Kessenich

Fiction

CINNAMON GIRL
North Star Press, September 2016

Poetry

**HARD TIMES REQUIRE
FURIOUS DANCING**
Big Table Publishing, August 2023

AGE OF WONDERS
Big Table Publishing, December 2015

BEFORE WHOSE GLORY
FutureCycle Press, February 2013

PEARL
Letterpress Book Publishing

Lawrence Kessenich

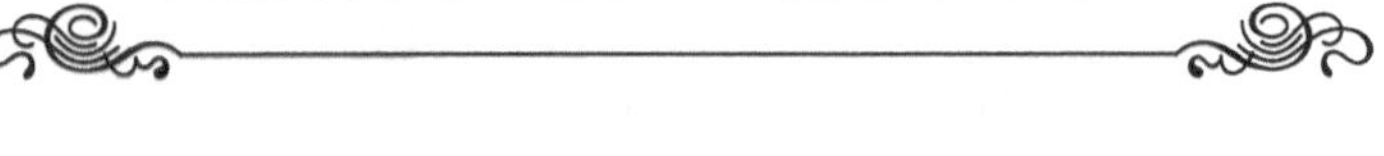

Kessenich is a fiction writer, poet, playwright, essayist, reviewer, and editor. His first novel, *Cinnamon Girl*, was published in 2016. He has also published some short stories and won the 2010 **Strokestown International Poetry Prize** in Ireland.

Kessenich has six books of poetry: ***Before Whose Glory***, ***Age of Wonders***, ***Hard Times Require Furious Dancing***, ***Strange News*** and ***Pearl***.

His short plays have been produced in New York, Boston, and in Colorado, where he won the **People's Choice Award** in a national drama competition. His full-length play, ***Anne Frank Lives!***, was performed at a festival in New York City. He has also published essays, one of which was featured on NPR's "This I Believe" and appears in the anthology ***This I Believe: On Love.***

Kessenich was born and raised in Wisconsin in a loving family with nine children. He attended St. Monica's grade school in Whitefish Bay, Messmer High School in the city of Milwaukee, and the University of Wisconsin-Milwaukee. He was also briefly in the graduate creative writing program at the University of Massachusetts-Amherst. After attending the Radcliffe Publishing Course, he spent 10 years in the trade editorial department at Houghton Mifflin in Boston, where he edited ***Shoeless Joe***, the basis for the movie ***Field of Dreams*** (in which he and his wife Janet appears onscreen as extras), and many other fiction and nonfiction books.

Since leaving book publishing, Kessenich has made his living first as a technical writer and then as a marketing writer. He has also taught classes on writing and book publishing. He lives in the Boston area and is happy to consider readings, speaking engagements, workshops, and writing and editing work.